BOOKS BY CHRISTIE HARRIS

Confessions of a Toe-Hanger
Figleafing Through History *(With Moira Johnston)*
Forbidden Frontier
Let X Be Excitement
Mouse Woman and the Mischief-Makers
Mouse Woman and the Muddleheads
Mouse Woman and the Vanished Princesses
Once Upon a Totem
Once More Upon a Totem
Raven's Cry
Secret in the Stlalakum Wild
Sky Man on the Totem Pole?
West with the White Chiefs
You Have to Draw the Line Somewhere

Mouse Woman and the Muddleheads

Mouse Woman and the Muddleheads

by

CHRISTIE HARRIS

all the best to Vicki
Christie Harris
(I feel I know you)

DRAWINGS BY DOUGLAS TAIT

McClelland & Stewart

1979

Published in the United States by
Atheneum Publishers, New York
Published simultaneously in Canada by
McClelland & Stewart, Ltd.
25 Hollinger Road, Toronto
ISBN 0-7710-3984-0
Manufactured by
Halliday Lithograph Corporation
West Hanover, Massachusetts
First Edition

TO

the native people of the Northwest Coast

who gave us Mouse Woman

Contents

Mouse Woman and the Muddleheads

Before You Read the Stories

It was in the time of very long ago, when things were different.

Then supernatural beings roamed the seas and the vast green wildernesses of the Northwest Coast. The people called them narnauks. And everyone was very, very careful not to anger the narnauks.

In those days the people lived in totem pole villages that stood with their backs to the big, snowcapped mountains. The villages were bright with the carved and painted emblems of the clans: Eagle, Raven, Bear, Wolf, Frog. . . . Always fronting on the water where the totem-crested canoes were drawn up, they edged many lonely beaches; they fringed certain bays along the rivers.

The people fished the rivers. They hunted the hills and the seas. And when winter came, they feasted in their enormous cedar houses and settled the affairs of the people. Wearing colorful regalia, they drummed and chanted and danced; they told stories.

In the stories there were many well-known characters. One of these was Mouse Woman, a tiny narnauk who watched the world with her big, busy, mouse eyes. Because she was a spirit being, Mouse Woman could appear as a mouse or as the tiniest of grandmothers; or she could move about without any body. Also because she was a spirit being, any gifts she received should have been transformed into their essence, by fire, for her use. But the mouse in Mouse Woman was so strong that sometimes—if the gifts were woolen—she snatched them up before they were more than scorched. And her ravelly little fingers began tearing them into lovely, loose, nesty piles of wool. It was the one improper delight of a very, very proper little being.

Mouse Woman liked everyone and everything to be proper. To her, anyone who couldn't see that the proper way to do things was the *only* way to do things, was a Muddlehead. And she had little patience with Muddleheads. In fact, because she was the busiest little busybody in the Place of Supernatural Beings, she often did something about the Muddleheads.

What she did is told in these stories.

The Mink Being Who Wanted to Marry a Princess

It was in the time of very long ago, when things were different.

Mouse Woman, looking like the tiniest of tiny grandmothers, was scurrying along the trail. Her eyes were flashing with annoyance. Her nose was twitching. "Muddlehead!" she kept squeaking.

It was the kind of muddleheadedness she had run into before. And being the busiest little busybody in the Place of Supernatural Beings, she intended to do something about it.

"Why do narnauks ever want to marry human princesses?" she asked herself in furious little squeaks. They knew it led to nothing but trouble. "Muddlehead!" she burst out again.

Slow Mink was the muddlehead she was annoyed with at the moment. *He* wanted to marry a human princess. A stupid thing to want! But then, Slow Mink was one of the stupidest narnauks in the Place. And what made it worse was that his mother doted on him. She thought that, in his human form, he was such an extraordinarily handsome fellow that any young lady would *want* to marry him. Clearly, she was not at all bright either.

"So there you are, Slow Mink!" Mouse Woman said when she finally found him, alone and in his human form. He was rather handsome, she admitted. And the robe hanging from his shoulders was truly elegant. "But you can't marry a human princess!" she burst out.

"Well . . . if I do . . . I can," he slowly pointed out, blinking from the effort of remembering what it was that his mother had told him. "I think," he added, not being at all that sure of just what she had told him.

"Then you're not going to," Mouse Woman said. "Humans are very particular about their princesses, since *they* carry the royal bloodlines. They'd never approve of a marriage with a narnauk."

"Well . . . if they didn't know I was a narnauk . . ." he said, still blinking to remember what it was that his mother had told him. "If I pretended to be just a human . . ."

"Then they'd want to know all about you—your rank, your family, your wealth and so on.

Go and see for yourself how it is with a human princess!"

"If . . . you say so," he agreed. And he vanished on the spot.

"I didn't mean right now," Mouse Woman called after the now invisible narnauk. "Muddle-head!" she squeaked. Then, just to keep an eye on things, she became invisible herself as she followed him. And she frowned an invisible frown when she discovered which village he was making for. "That mother of his!" she burst out.

IT WAS A BEAUTIFUL VILLAGE, with totem-decorated cedar houses and poles standing with their backs to a forested mountain. In front of the houses, totem-crested canoes were drawn up along the beach.

At the moment, four canoes were moving in from another village. They were big, Wolf-crested canoes filled with people dressed in ceremonial robes and headdresses. They were coming in with a chanting and a ceremonial flourish of paddles to show the greatness of their Wolf Clan, and the greatness of their Wolf Prince, who stood high on a plank that had been laid across the leading canoe.

"Another suitor for the Eagle Princess!" people on shore were exclaiming to one another. "Another suitor to be rejected!"

So many suitors had come to the village to ask

for the beautiful Eagle Princess—only to be rejected!—that even she was becoming annoyed.

"You'll never find someone to suit you!" she stormed at her mother, who was watching the approaching canoes with disdain. For, of course, in the way of the Northern People, only Eagles could arrange a marriage for the Eagle Princess; and in this matrilineal society, it was her mother and her maternal uncles who were of the Eagle crest, like herself. "You'll never let anyone marry me!" she stormed at her mother and her maternal uncles.

"Oh . . . when a young man worthy of you appears . . ." her mother assured her.

". . . you'll send him home, too," the princess predicted. And she eyed the handsome Wolf Prince with wistful eyes. She had seen him before, at a feast; and she had dreamed dreams about him.

"YOU SEE?" Mouse Woman said to Slow Mink when they were back at the Place once more. "You can't marry a human princess!"

"Well . . . if I do . . . I can," he stubbornly repeated, blinking as before. And he went off to see his doting mother.

"How shall I go to the village?" he asked her. "With four canoes full of chanting relatives?"

"Well . . ." his mother hedged; for his narnauk relatives would certainly never agree to go to the village to ask for the princess. And even if they could somehow bring themselves to do such an unheard-of thing, they'd never do it for Slow Mink. He just was not appreciated by the Mink People, who were probably jealous of his handsome face and form, his mother thought. They seemed unwilling to arrange a marriage for him with one of their own daughters. Which was why she was encouraging him to find a human princess. "Perhaps we shall have to trick the human," she told him, as she had told him before.

Slow Mink agreed. He always agreed with his mother. And that very night he appeared to the princess, who had angrily escaped from her hovering attendants. He appeared as a handsome young man wearing a truly elegant mink robe.

"I came to marry you," he said simply, since simply was the only way he knew how to speak.

"Good!" the young lady answered, with flashing eyes. If she disappeared with this rather handsome fellow, she thought, it would startle her family into finally arranging a *proper* marriage for her. He had no ear ornaments to denote high rank, she noticed; so probably he was just a handsome upstart. But she wouldn't actually go far with him. Just far enough to alarm her family.

Only, it didn't work out that way. When she took his hand, the princess found herself powerless to break away from her suitor. There was something strange about him, too, she realized, apart from his lack of ear ornaments. There was something unnatural, something eerie. And by the time he led her down the trail into the Place of Supernatural Beings, she was as alarmed as she had intended her family to be.

The Place was different from all the villages she knew. It was at the bottom of a valley ringed by high cliffs topped with a jungle of devil's club. Animals as well as people were moving in and out of the houses. She even caught a glimpse of a monster. A monster with two heads!

The young man stopped in front of a house decorated with Mink totems.

"Mink?" she thought, swallowing. She knew of no people with Mink as their family crest. Glancing fearfully about, she saw that all the houses were carved and painted with unfamiliar totems.

"Did you get what you went for?" a woman's voice called out from somewhere deep inside Mink House.

"Yes . . . I got . . . what I went for," the young man answered. "I think," he added.

"Then bring in my daughter-in-law!" the voice ordered.

"Daughter-in-law!" the princess gasped. "But—I can't marry anyone until proper arrangements have been made by my family." Her voice was a scared whisper by the time it got to the "family."

"Bring in my daughter-in-law!"

The young man led her inside. And the interior of the big, windowless house did nothing to lessen her alarm. It was dimly lit by a fire that cast fantastic shadows. And who knew what monsters might be lurking in the corners where the light did not reach? There *were* people. But the people were not sitting, or working, as people should be sitting, or working. These people were prowling around as restlessly as some minks who were also prowling around, each by himself or herself. The princess swallowed, several times.

"Sit by the fire, my dear!" the voice ordered.

Now the frightened girl saw that the speaker was a woman wearing a gorgeous mink robe, a woman who paused only long enough to indicate a mat by the fire. Then she was off again, prowling.

The young man, too, began prowling.

While she was looking fearfully about her, the princess felt a tug at her woolen robe. And there stood the tiniest of tiny grandmothers.

"Mouse Woman!" she gasped. For this could only be Mouse Woman, the tiny narnauk who was known to be a friend to young people who'd been tricked into trouble. "Grandmother!" she whispered gratefully, glancing anxiously about to see that no one else had noticed.

"Do you know whose house this is?" Mouse Woman demanded. And her fingers seemed almost to nibble at the wool in the girl's robe.

"N . . . no, Grandmother."

"This is the house of the Mink People." The big, busy mouse eyes were watching the swing of the girl's wool-and-abalone ear ornaments. "Throw them into the fire, my dear!" she ordered, indicating the earrings.

The princess wasted no time. For it was well known that Mouse Woman was a stickler for proper behavior. If help were to be given, something must be given in return. Quickly she threw her ear ornaments into the fire to transform them into their essence for use by the little spirit being.

But before they were more than scorched, Mouse Woman snatched them out of the fire and her ravelly little fingers began tearing them into a lovely, loose, nesty pile of mountain sheep wool. Then, having received her favorite gift, she proceeded to give her favorite giving—advice to a young person in trouble.

"First, get Slow Mink away from his mother!" she advised the princess. "Then remember that he is stupid! And then do what you must do!" She vanished as mother and son came back to the fire.

"Now you will be married, my dear," Mink Woman said.

"Oh . . . yes!" the princess agreed, as soon as she could find her wits and her voice. "I will be married as soon as I can persuade my family to arrange the marriage." She meant the marriage with the handsome Wolf Prince.

"You think you can persuade your family?" Mink Woman asked, watching the girl with narrowed eyes. For, of course, she would have preferred to have her precious son married with ceremony.

"I'm sure I can persuade them," the princess said. After this alarm, even *her* family would swiftly arrange a proper marriage for her. "He is such a handsome suitor!" Again she meant the Wolf Prince.

First, get Slow Mink away from his mother! Mouse Woman had said.

"Perhaps your son could take me home so that I could start talking to my family?" the princess suggested. And she almost held her breath for the answer because she did not know the way home.

Mink Woman looked at her with quick, bright eyes. "No," she decided. "Not until I've had time to think about it." And off she went, to prowl around the firelight with her shadow, which kept changing into monstrous shapes.

"No. Not until she's had time to think about it," Slow Mink echoed, fixing his mother's decision firmly in his mind. Then he, too, turned to begin prowling.

This time the princess caught his luxurious robe. "Can't we walk by ourselves . . . outside?" she suggested. "Then I can find out more about you." She wanted to find out just how stupid he was.

"If . . . you say so," he agreed. "I . . . could take you to my fishing den."

"Oh, do take me to your fishing den!" she urged

him. Anything to get him away from his mother, as Mouse Woman had advised. But what could he be planning to fish for? After all, winter was just ending. The first fish of the year, the Salvation Fish—the crowding tribes of tiny silver oolachans—had not yet moved into the Nass River. Indeed, her people had been waiting for the signal before she had left the village. By now, any who were not out searching for her might well be on their way to the Nass River.

"Perhaps . . ." she whispered to herself, in sudden hope. Perhaps his fishing den was along the Nass, where she could find her family!

But he did not take her to the Nass. In an eerie, gliding way he took her along unfamiliar mountain trails and unfamiliar mountain creeks until they reached the sea. The sea! But which way was home? the princess wondered, glancing to the north and to the south for a familiar landmark. But she saw none.

"I catch eels," Slow Mink told her as he lifted a rock in a tidal pool. He snatched up a dark slithery little creature. "Here!" He handed the eel to the princess.

"Oh! It's slippery!" she cried out, dropping it. The princess did not like eels.

Slow Mink did. Obviously. He gulped down dozens of the dark slithery little creatures while they were still alive and wriggling. He kept offering them to the princess.

"I don't like eels," she kept telling him. Also, she had no intention of eating anything a narnauk might offer her. She had heard too many tales of captured princesses being turned into narnauks themselves through eating what they were offered. Until she found a way to escape back to her own people, she would survive by chewing the bits of mountain goat fat in the pouch at her waist.

Which way was home?

Stubbornly resolved not to let her go home until his mother had had time to think about it, Slow Mink would never tell her, she knew. But perhaps. . . . Her eyes widened with an idea. Perhaps he would take her to the Nass River. She began to watch him closely to discover how she could trick him.

Clearly, he was eager to please her so that she *would* persuade her family to let her marry him with ceremony. Clearly, he was concerned not to anger her.

Every day he went out to catch eels in the tidal pools. Every day he came back with a big basket full of the dark slithery little creatures for his supper, and also with several strings of eels—strung twenty to a string on cedar withes—to smoke for later eating. And after he had hung the strings of fresh eels up in the smoke to dry, he always counted the eels that had already been smoked. He counted them loudly, checking each eel against a toe or a finger. "One. And another one. And another one . . ."

"It always comes out even with toes and fingers!" he cried out in never-ending surprise at the rightness of the strings of smoked eels. Then he always ate his supper, gulping down eels that were still alive and wriggling. And while she watched him eat, the princess always felt a little less hungry than she felt at other times.

"Why do you count the eels?" she finally asked him.

"Because it always comes out even with toes and fingers," he told her.

"Or because you think I might have taken some of them?" she asked, pretending to be angry.

"Oh no, no, no, no!" he assured her. "You don't like eels. So you wouldn't take them. I count them because it always comes out even with toes and fingers . . . I think," he added.

The princess narrowed her eyes. She chewed her mountain goat fat, growing more and more determined to trick him into helping her find her people.

The very next morning, as soon as he had left for the tidal pools, she slipped several eels—now stiff as sticks—off each of the strings of smoked eels. These she hid in a corner.

By and by, Slow Mink came back with the big basket full of the dark slithery little creatures for his supper, and also with three strings of eels to smoke for later eating. These he hung up in the smoke, as always. Then, as always, he began to count the eels that had already been smoked. He counted the first string loudly, checking each eel against a toe or a finger.

But! This time, something was wrong. He had three toes left over. "It doesn't come out even with toes and fingers!" he cried out. Then he counted another string. And this time he had four toes left over. "This one doesn't come out even, either!" he cried out in dismay. "Maybe somebody ate them."

"I suppose you think I ate them," the princess said, pretending to be very angry.

"Oh no, no, no, no!" he assured her. "You don't like eels. You didn't eat them. So maybe I ate them myself." He blinked and scratched his head, trying to remember. Then he ran a hand over his stomach. "No, I didn't eat them," he decided. "Or my stomach would be fuller."

"Then someone is doing something to confuse you," the princess said, with truth. "Perhaps we had better leave while you still have plenty of smoked eels to eat on the journey."

"What journey?" Slow Mink asked her, blinking to remember if his mother had said anything about a journey.

"The journey to find food I can eat, of course," she answered. "Or do you want me to die? . . . If I die," she wailed, "how can I persuade my family to let me marry?"

Slow Mink blinked and scratched his head and thought about it.

"You want me to die," she said, pretending to be very, very angry.

"Oh, no, no, no, no!" he assured her. "I don't want you to die."

"Then find food that I can eat! Find fresh fish!"

"Fresh fish?" he said, blinking; for even he knew there were no salmon running in the rivers at this time of the year.

"The Salvation Fish?" she suggested, as if that idea had just struck her. "But I suppose you won't take me to the Nass River because you do want me to die."

"Oh no, no, no, no! I'll take you to the Nass," he said, still blinking, still scratching his head, but no longer really thinking about it. After all, now that his mother was not around to tell him what to do, he was no doubt glad to have someone else telling him what to do.

So it was that they set off the very next morning, taking the strings of dried eels with them. In an eerie, gliding way, Slow Mink led her along unfamiliar trails and creeks until they reached the familiar Nass River.

Here, the sun was shining on ice rimming the river; eagles were circling overhead; and far downriver there was the bellowing of the sea lions who—like the seals and the sea gulls and the people—were following the crowding tribes of tiny silver oolachans into the river. The Salvation Fish were coming! And some of her people, she knew, would already be at their camping place upriver, ready to rake in the silver harvest.

Then a group of canoes appeared from around a bend, moving upriver ahead of the fish. And with the wariness of her people, the princess hid behind a tree while she found out who it was coming.

It was not her own people. Leading the fleet of canoes were high-ranking strangers who wore ear and nose ornaments of white bone.

"What are those white things?" Slow Mink asked her when the canoes had passed by. He was feeling his own ears and nose to notice that he had no such things growing on them.

"Oh, those are their ear and nose ornaments. Bones," she told him; and she narrowed her eyes with a sudden idea. "Those are to show their high rank. If they didn't wear them, how could anyone know they were chiefs and chieftainesses, princes and princesses?"

"You don't wear them," Slow Mink noted, looking at her bare earlobes and her bare nose.

"I was wearing ear ornaments when you found me," she reminded him. "I . . . must have lost them somewhere." She had no intention of telling him that *her* ear ornaments had been given to Mouse Woman in return for the information that *he* was stupid. "See! My earlobes have been pierced for earrings. Every high ranking person's ears are pierced for ornaments . . . Oh dear!" she said, as though in sudden dismay. She examined his earlobes with apparent concern. "My family will never think you are high ranking enough to marry me. You have no ear ornaments. Oh dear! Oh dear!"

"I . . . could have," he said slowly, blinking and scratching his head and thinking about it.

"How could you, with no holes in your earlobes?" she wailed.

"Well . . . I could have holes . . . I think," he answered.

"Of course you *could,*" the princess hastened to assure him. "I suppose . . . I could pierce them for you myself. After all, I do want to marry a handsome suitor." She was thinking of the handsome Wolf Prince. And she certainly did want to marry him.

. . . *remember that he is stupid!* Mouse Woman had said. *And then do what you must do!*

At long last, she knew what she must do to escape from this Mink Being and get back to her family.

"How do they make the holes?" Slow Mink asked her, feeling his earlobes.

"Well . . ." The princess swallowed. "They . . . sharpen a hard spruce branch to a point and drive it through the earlobe. So, if you want to wear ear ornaments to show your high rank to my family, you must sharpen a hard spruce branch." She took her little woman's knife from her pouch. But Slow Mink had a bigger knife.

"Now, get the hard spruce branch!" she told him.

He blinked several times and scratched his head, thinking about it. But he did get the hard spruce branch.

"Now sharpen it to a point!" she told him. And when he had done that, she said, "Where is your stone hammer?"

He produced the stone hammer.

"Now lie down on this wide log so that I will have something to drive against!"

"But it's going to hurt," he protested.

"Oh well, if you aren't interested in being of high enough rank to marry me . . ." she said, turning as if to leave him.

Slow Mink lay down on the wide log.

"Now close your eyes!" the princess advised, wishing she could close her eyes too.

"But I'll die!" he protested.

"Did those people die?" she challenged him. "Did I die?"

"No," he said, after he had thought about it.

"Then put your ear close to the log!"

"But—"

"Oh, if you're afraid . . ." she said. "I certainly can't marry a man who wears no ornaments of high rank. That's not proper for a princess."

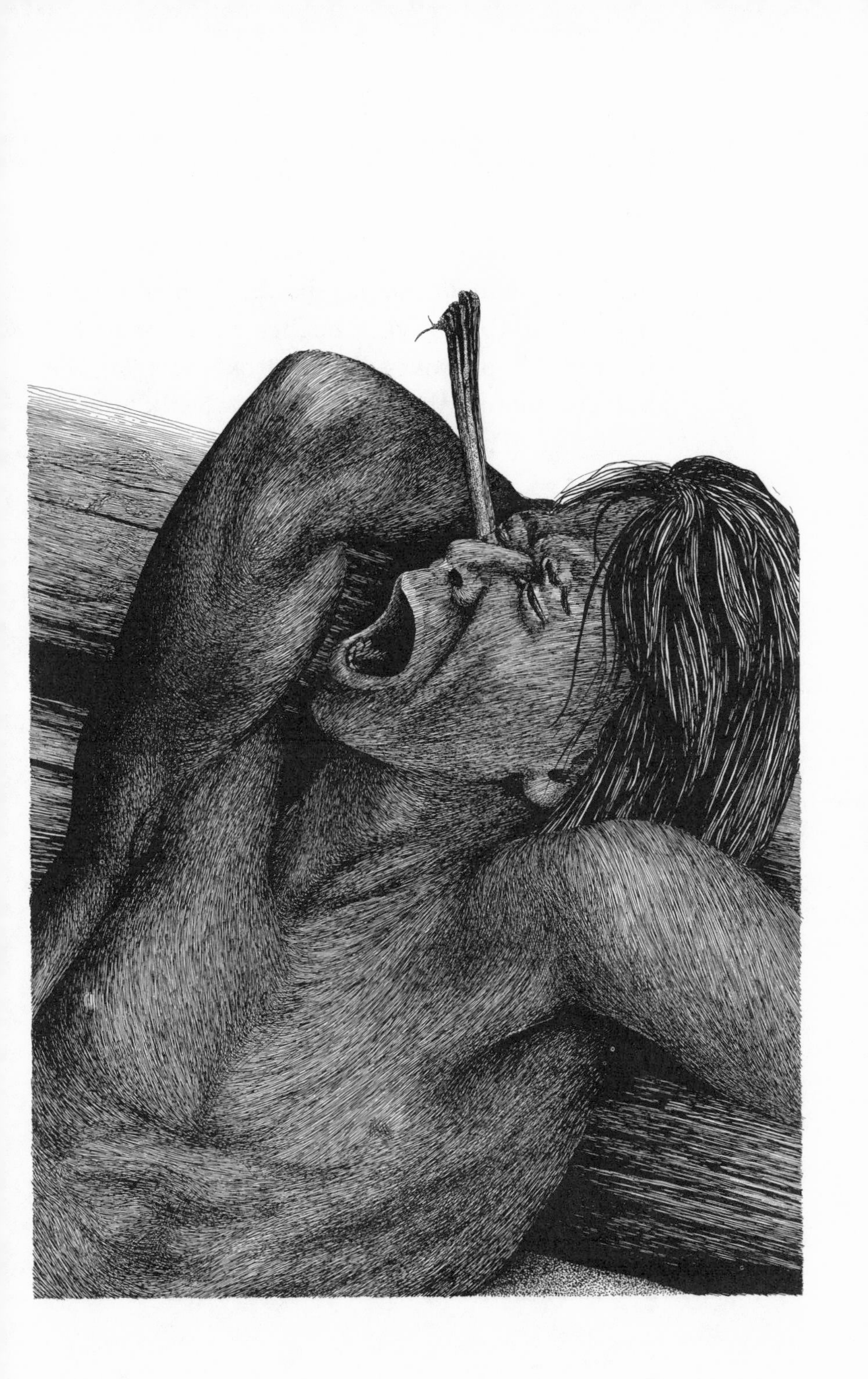

He put his right ear down close to the log. Then he closed his eyes.

Shuddering at what she *must* do, the princess held the point of the sharpened branch against his earlobe. She gave a mighty stroke with the hammer. Two strokes. Three strokes, driving the branch well into the log while Slow Mink howled with pain. Then, dropping the hammer, she fled upriver.

"I'm going to find my family and make them arrange the marriage," she called back to him. And her eyes flashed. Indeed she was going to make them arrange the marriage—the marriage with the Wolf Prince. If she could handle a narnauk, she could certainly handle her family.

SLOW MINK was still lying there, howling with pain, when Mouse Woman appeared to him.

"Muddlehead!" she cried out in furious little squeaks. "I told you you couldn't marry a human princess."

"You . . . ow . . . told me," he agreed. "And I'll . . . ow . . . tell my mother." That he didn't want to marry a human princess after all. "It . . . ow . . . hurts too much."

"Well, pull it out!" Mouse Woman ordered. She spirited herself up onto the log to help him.

"But . . . ow . . . the princess will be sad . . . ow . . . when she brings her family . . . ow . . . and finds me gone," he said as they got the hard spruce branch out of his earlobe. "I think," he added.

"Oh, don't worry about the princess!" Mouse Woman told him. "She'll find another husband."

And of course she did.

After the alarm of her disappearance and the horror of her capture by a narnauk, she had no trouble at all getting her family to arrange a marriage for her with the handsome Wolf Prince.

"If people weren't so muddleheaded about marriages!" Mouse Woman squeaked to herself as she scurried home from the wedding.

The Sea Hunters Who Were Swallowed by a Whirlpool

NOTHING MUDDLED a man's head more than ambition, Mouse Woman decided one day when she was thinking about a certain young sea hunter who wanted to become a great chief.

It was in the time of very, very long ago. In fact, it was just after the Flood, when people were scattered all over the coast, far from their old familiar villages.

One large family group had found refuge on an offshore island. They had survived the Flood with a good supply of provisions. But since they didn't know what had happened to their old fishing stations, their old clam beaches, their old mountain goat hunting grounds or their old berry patches, they were anxious to find new sources of food.

"There are still sea lions and sea otters and seals out there in the ocean," said the ambitious young sea hunter, who had a long name that meant Dragging-Along-Shore. "The Flood hasn't destroyed *them.*"

Like most of the men in the group, he was of the Killer Whale Crest. And with many of the old chiefs lost in the Flood along with their true heirs, it was a time for ambitious young Killer Whales to prove their worth and win entitlement to the now empty chieftainships.

"Perhaps several canoes can go out, in different directions," he suggested. With his skill, of course, *he* would find the most food and could then claim leadership among the survivors.

For his canoe, he carefully selected the two most stalwart young paddlers in the group—Killer Whales like himself. He frowned at a third young man, Holdamia, who wore Eagle tattoes. Holdamia, his sister's husband, was a superb canoeman. His eyes would be able to read the changed currents and the menace of newly submerged rocks along a coastline now changed beyond belief. But Holdamia was not a Killer Whale. Still, the ambitious young man thought, only the best would do as steersman on this important and hazardous venture. "You will steer the canoe!" he told Holdamia.

Because they might be out on the sea for many days, they took some of the precious mountain goat fat, dried salmon, dried cranberries and oolachan oil to mix with the dried foods. And because they might have to appease angry ocean beings, they also took along a valuable copper as a gift, and a small basket of eagle down—the symbol of peace and friendship—to waft reverently over troubled waters.

For three days they paddled and paddled, and found nothing. On the fourth day, Dragging-Along-Shore said, "It's useless to hunt here. We'll turn back." He was angry because all his skill as a sea hunter had come to nothing, while lesser rivals might already have found animals in other directions. "Turn back at once!" he ordered the steersman.

They turned back. And when evening came, they found themselves in a channel, with a mountain rising steeply on the mainland side.

"Let's anchor here for the night," the weary steersman suggested.

Dragging-Along-Shore agreed.

Holdamia cast his heavy anchor stone overboard at the foot of a sheer rock cliff. And the weary men pulled their blankets up over them to get some much needed sleep.

Now, AS IT HAPPENED, the unlucky sea hunters had stopped right over the undersea house of a Supernatural Being called Na-gun-aks. In fact, their anchor stone hit his roof.

When it hit his roof, Na-gun-aks ordered one

of his female slaves to go out and see what the noise on his roof was all about.

To do this, the slave took on her animal form; and as a small blue cod, she swam up to the surface of the sea, to where the men were already asleep in their canoe. To see them, she had to leap up several times, right out of the water.

The noise disturbed Dragging-Along-Shore, who was not yet soundly asleep. For an instant he thought it was a sea lion or a sea otter or a seal. But when he discovered that it was only a small blue cod, he became very angry.

"You are mocking me!" he snapped at the leaping fish. With a quick lunge, he caught her. "You want me to look ridiculous," he said, "returning to my people with one tiny fish." In his anger, he smashed her fins and threw her back into the water. "Now you will not disturb my sleep again!" he shouted after her. Then he yanked his blanket up over his head and immediately went back to sleep.

Holdamia, who had been roused by the angry voice, looked at his brother-in-law with dismay. Lack of respect for any creature—however small—could bring nothing but trouble.

SWIMMING WITH PAIN and difficulty, the little blue cod made her way back to the house under the sea. And when she resumed her human form again, she was a cripple with broken bones. She wept as she poured out her story to her master.

"Bring the canoe down to my house!" Na-gun-aks roared to his people. And at once a whirlpool rose up to bring down the canoe.

It all happened so suddenly that only the steersman was really awake when the canoe came to rest on a high platform at the rear of a strange house. He shook the canoe to alert his comrades. "Alas! We are in danger," he whispered to them.

The others blinked their eyes and looked about them. They saw a huge, dimly lit house carved with sea creatures and hung with seaweeds. They saw a chief sitting at the rear of the fire, in front of the captured canoe. He wore a Killer Whale robe set all over with horns and a Killer Whale hat also covered with horns. And he was as big as the biggest of killer whales. Clearly, he was a Killer Whale monster.

When he spoke, his voice was as startling as the screaming whistle of a whole pod of killer whales. "Let my guests come down to the fire!" he commanded.

Terrified and half stunned by what had happened to them, the four humans stumbled down to the fire.

No sooner were they seated on the mats than Dragging-Along-Shore felt something touch him. Glancing down, he saw Mouse Woman, who held up a cautioning finger. Swiftly he moved his robe to be sure she was hidden from the monster.

"Throw your ear ornaments into the fire!" she ordered in small but imperious squeaks.

Thankful for a friend, Dragging-Along-Shore threw his woolen ear ornaments into the fire.

But before they were more than scorched, Mouse Woman snatched them out again and began tearing at the wool with her ravelly little fingers. And now, having received her favorite gift, she proceeded to give, in return, her favorite giving—advice to someone in trouble. "Do you know in whose house you are?" she demanded.

"No," the sea hunter whispered.

"This is the house of Chief Na-gun-aks. Your anchor stone hit his roof. He sent out a female slave to see what had caused the noise. She went out as a little blue cod. And *you* broke her fins. She was crippled and crying when she came back. So the chief sent a whirlpool up to capture you. . . . Now! I advise you to make recompense. Offer him whatever you have in the canoe to appease his anger!"

Almost before her squeaky voice stopped, Mouse Woman vanished into thin air. The sea, after all, was none of her business, as her fellow narnauks so often reminded her. And the busiest of little busybodies had other things to attend to.

Dragging-Along-Shore thought with dismay of his precious provisions. Not only would he have no new food to take back to the people to prove his worth, he would have lost all he had taken from the group's stores. Nevertheless, he quickly offered everything as a gift to the enormous Chief. Survival was his ambition at the moment.

Na-gun-aks accepted the gift. "Berries!" he cried out in his screaming whistle, and he smacked his enormous lips. He ground the dried berries between his enormous conical teeth. For, as was well known, the sea beings were very, very fond of berries. Then he commanded, "Boil some seals that I may feed my guests!"

The sea hunters trembled. Who knew what would happen to men who ate the food of supernatural beings? Yet they did not dare to refuse to eat the boiled seal. Yet after they ate, nothing seemed to happen. Everything stayed the same. They lived in a strange, vague, suspended way. And without the sun and the moon, the day and the night, the tides and the seasons, they had no way of knowing the passage of time. Anyway, they thought in a sort of dreamy despair, what did it matter? They would never go home again.

Only Holdamia, eating most sparingly, vaguely suspected that Na-gun-aks was sorry for the poor human beings who had survived the Flood, and that he favored Dragging-Along-Shore as the survivor most likely to provide him with the berries every Sea Being craved. Only Holdamia drowzily realized that Na-gun-aks liked company.

Yet even he was not prepared for the monstrous company that arrived one day, or one night.

That day, or that night, the chief ordered the humans to climb up into the canoe that was still resting on the high platform at the rear of the house.

They did this as if they were in a dream, and then watched as the door of the enormous undersea house opened long enough to let in murky water, turbulent with the movements of gigantic bodies. Shrinking back and huddling together in bewilderment, the men watched until the movements of the gigantic bodies had stilled. Then they peered stupidly into the murky water, aware of vague, shadowy, monstrous shapes.

The stillness was shattered by a screaming whistle.

"Look well at my human guests!" Na-gun-aks shrieked at the unseen beings. "Do not upset their canoes when they go again on the waters!"

Because Na-gun-aks wants the berries in those canoes for himself, Holdamia thought in a vague, drowsy way.

Na-gun-aks' words reached the other men as if from a dream. . . . *when they go again on the waters!* Their eyes stayed listless and waiting, as though the hopeful words had not been said.

Again the stillness was cut by a screaming whistle.

"Now! My human guests must see you!"

As the stupefied men looked on, some of the murky water flowed out of the enormous undersea house. And heads appeared above the lowered water—monstrous heads with bulging fish eyes . . . and spurting blowholes . . . and waving tentacles . . . and cavernous mouths. . . .

Shuddering as though half-waking from a dreadful dream, the terrified humans resolved to be even more respectful at sea than they had been before the Flood. Now that they had seen what was lurking down there in the cold, mysterious depths of the ocean, they would always be ready with gifts of berries and mountain goat fat; they would always be ready to waft eagle down reverently over troubled waters; they would never, never, never spit in the sea. They huddled even closer together as Na-gun-aks had food and gifts distributed among the monstrous beings.

Then—at long last!—the door of the enormous undersea house opened; and the murky water flowed out, carrying off the terrifying company.

"Come down to the fire!" Na-gun-aks commanded.

Moving still like sleepwalkers, the men made their way down to the fire, dreamily surprised that somehow the fire was still blazing; the mats were still dry on the oozy ocean floor.

"Stand before me!" Na-gun-aks ordered Dragging-Along-Shore. He placed a Killer Whale Hat-set-with-horns on the sea hunter's head, while attendants dropped a garment of seaweeds over the young man's shoulders.

"I have something else to give you," the chief told him; and now his screaming whistle was like a terrible warning. "I give you a TABOO. Never again will you harm a fish! You will take fish only when they offer themselves to you by floating up to the surface!" He turned his monstrous head several times to glare at the young sea hunter with each of his killer whale eyes. *"You shall have great good fortune in sea hunting. As long as you do it with respect.* And to keep my favor, you will come often above my house and offer gifts to me. Especially BERRIES!"

Speaking as though in his sleep, the sea hunter vowed to cherish Na-gun-aks' favor. Always, he vowed, always he would honor his taboo. Never, never, never would he harm a fish. *You shall have great good fortune in sea hunting.* The words seemed to float about the ambitious young man's ears. *You shall have great good fortune in sea hunting.* Dragging-Along-Shore smiled as though he had had a wonderful dream.

"Now go to sleep in your canoe!"

The men stumbled back to their canoe. And soon they were fast asleep.

Again it was the steersman who woke up first. Terrified! For there was a mountain of foam around the canoe. "Wake up!" he cried out, shaking the canoe to rouse his comrades. "Alas! We are in danger!" He was as alert, now, as he had ever been.

As the men watched, trembling with dread at

the strange thing that was happening to them, the foam changed into a fog, a fog so thick that they could not see one another. Perhaps they had awakened in the Land of Ghosts? Then there was a crashing roll of thunder. Each held his breath, waiting for what was to happen next. But the fog began to thin. The sun broke through, showing them the channel with a mountain rising steeply on the mainland side. They were anchored at the foot of the sheer rock cliff. As if nothing strange had ever happened.

Every man sagged with relief. Then looked about in dismay. For they and their canoe were covered with barnacles and seaweed and sea anenome, with tangles of kelp tubes and sea-shells. Glistening wet green and brown sea ribbons streamed over Dragging-Along-Shore's Killer Whale Hat-set-with-horns, and down over his garment of seaweed. They and their canoe were engulfed in marine growth, like a tidal rock.

"Take up your paddles and get away from this spot!" Dragging-Along-Shore commanded in a hoarse whisper.

But the paddles were almost too heavy to lift. And through the barnacles and seaweed and sea anenome and tangles of kelp tubes and sea shells, the startled men caught the gleam of copper. When one of the paddles touched the side of the canoe, there was a deep, metallic DONG.

Too stunned even to wipe the seaweed from

their faces, the men gasped as the copper canoe took off. Faster than a killer whale could swim, it made straight for the island they seemed to have left only a few days before. It stopped offshore, in front of the refugee village.

HOLDAMIA'S WIFE, the sister of the chief sea hunter, was walking sadly along the beach, singing her mourning song, when she saw the strange sight.

"A sea monster!" she cried out, racing toward a house.

People rushed out to see. Cowering close to the buildings and to one another, they looked fearfully at the thing out on the water.

Something moved in the tangle of seaweeds. And a voice called out, "Was not a chief sea hunter lost from this village with his men?"

"Yes!" the people called back. "A year ago." They almost held their breath as more things moved in the tangle of seaweeds. They cringed and huddled together at the sudden DONG that came from the thing.

"Well, we are home again!" Dragging-Along-Shore sang out.

And now the people saw that it was, indeed, a canoe—a canoe covered with barnacles and seaweed and sea anenome and tangles of kelp tubes and sea shells. They caught the glint of copper through the engulfing marine growth.

"Holdamia! Dragging-Along-Shore!" the young

woman cried out, now with joy. She raced to the beach, with the others close behind her.

It took all the men in the village to bring the copper canoe ashore; while the women watched with a mingling of joy and terror and bewilderment. What could have happened to the sea hunters? What could have happened to their cedar canoe?

"What happened?" they asked. And now their voices were hushed with wonder. "What happened?"

Dragging-Along-Shore opened his mouth to tell them. *You shall have great good fortune in sea hunting!* The words were singing in his heart. And, surging once more with ambition, he raised his arms for silence. Here was undreamed of glory. Here, under the special favor of a supernatural being, was a future greater than any he could have dreamed of.

"Call in the people!" he said. "Send messengers to all other survivors you have found! And ask the chiefs to wear their great crests!" Only ceremonial splendor could do proper honor to the tale he would tell them, as only publicly naming his relatives *The People of Na-gun-aks* could ensure the continuing favor of the supernatural being.

When the assembled people were seated around the fire in their proudest regalia, Dragging-Along-Shore told them what had happened. He showed them his Killer-Whale-Hat-set-with-horns and his seaweed garment. He told them of his taboo.

The marveling and the feasting lasted for many days.

Then Dragging-Along-Shore began to go out on the water. And now, with the special favor of Na-gun-aks, he became the greatest of all the sea hunters along the coast, and the wealthiest, and the most honored, and the most swollen with pride.

Careful to keep the supernatural favor, he offered many gifts of berries to Na-gun-aks. He honored his taboo. But as his good fortune went on and on, as his fame spread along the coast, he began to grow careless. Although he himself would harm no fish, he was at no great pains to see that his men were mindful also, although their chief's taboo was *their* taboo, as well.

What was bound to happen, happened.

One day he had his brother-in-law with him as he was going to the channel to offer another gift of dried berries to Chief Na-gun-aks. As usual, sea lions and sea otters and seals came to him in abundance; fish floated up to him for the taking. And when evening came, he camped not far from the spot where they had once anchored their canoe at the foot of a sheer rock cliff. He would offer the gift the next morning, he told Holdamia as the two of them rested by the campfire.

His men were attending to the canoe when one of them saw a bullhead that had run aground and now lay panting at the water's edge. He moved toward it with a club.

Another man stopped him. "Our chief's taboo!" he reminded the first man. Then he went off to gather firewood.

"He's an ugly brute," the man with the club said to a friend; and he laughed at the wide mouth of the poor, panting fish.

"Not to other bullheads," his friend suggested; and he too laughed at the fish. "No doubt a wide mouth is a sign of beauty among bullheads."

"Then let us make him even more beautiful!" the man with the club said. He, once a superb fisherman, had been more and more frustrated by his chief's taboo. For what exhilaration was there in scooping up dead fish? Now he took out his knife. And while his laughing comrade held the poor bullhead, he cut its mouth wider at both sides.

They were still laughing at their cruel prank when the man came back with his firewood. "You foolish men!" he shouted at them. Aghast at this disrespect to a creature, and terrified of the menace of a broken taboo, he rushed to alert his chief. For, by ceremonial appeasement, Dragging-Along-Shore might be able to avert the disaster that was sure to follow the breaking of a taboo.

To his astonishment, his chief made no effort to avert the disaster.

Holdamia knew why.

In his heart, Dragging-Along-Shore knew that the fault was his own. Filled with his own fame, he had failed to be mindful enough of his crew's behavior. So his taboo had been broken. And now that it *had* been broken, Na-gun-aks' favor would be taken from him. Without the special favor of the sea being, he would no longer be the greatest of all the great sea hunting chiefs. And since he could not bear to live as anything less, he would gracefully accept the consequences of his broken taboo. *As the storytellers would remind generations of his people.*

"I have lived with honor. I will die with honor," he told Holdamia. "I will go with my men above Na-gun-aks' house this very evening. But this has nothing to do with you, an Eagle. You will not go with me."

Again Holdamia knew why.

If no one saw what happened, if no one survived to tell the tale, how would the storytellers ever know that Dragging-Along-Shore had indeed died with honor?

"We will go now. And you will climb that hill, where you will be able to see what happens to us when we have rounded the point and gone into the channel. Then you will go back and tell the people!"

So it was that Holdamia stood on the hill, watching, while the canoe rounded the point and went into the channel where a mountain rose steeply on the mainland side. He watched as the canoemen reached the spot at the foot of a sheer rock cliff. Then, with horror, he watched as a whirlpool spun the canoe and swallowed it as if it had been nothing but a bit of driftwood.

This time, Mouse Woman did nothing about it. Even the busiest little busybody in the Place would no nothing to help anyone who had broken a sacred taboo. And for all his fame, Dragging-Along-Shore was only a Muddlehead who had been used by an ocean being who craved a constant supply of berries.

Besides, as her fellow narnauks so often reminded her, the sea was none of her business.

Robin Woman and Sawbill Duck Woman

Always there were supernatural beings who wanted to marry a human, even though they knew that nothing but trouble ever came from such a union.

But once there was a human who wanted to marry a supernatural being. In fact, *two* supernatural beings.

"And perhaps he should!" Mouse Woman squeaked to herself. For anyone that muddle-headed needed to learn a thing or two. She began watching proceedings with her big, busy mouse eyes.

As it happened, the human, a handsome young chief, had no wife at all; though it was proper for a chief to have at least one wife, if not three or four wives. All his relatives were alert for a young lady he would be willing to marry. But they could find no one to suit him.

"You *must* have a wife!" they told him, again and again. It was only proper. And a chief, above all people, *must* do what was proper. "You must have a wife!" they insisted.

"Very well," he said, one fine autumn day. "I shall have a wife. In fact, *two* wives."

"Two wives?" they cried out in dismay. "Where shall we find two wives when we can't find even one to suit you?"

"Among the supernatural beings," he told them.

Their mouths dropped open. It was unheard of for a man to want to marry a supernatural being. As they promptly told the young chief.

"Nevertheless I shall marry two supernatural women," he told them. After all, as he explained to them, it would be a very fine thing for him and his people to have the marvelous aid of two supernatural beings. It would add even more luster to his already great prestige along the coast. And *his* prestige was *their* prestige, he reminded them.

They had to agree, though they still felt unsettled as they considered the matter.

"Since our hunters need spirit aid on land and on sea," he went on, "I shall marry a supernatural being from each area. Send out parties of hunters to find two such women! . . . Perhaps one of them could be Robin Woman," he added; and his eyes grew wistful. For he had heard of the beauty of the Robin Princess.

After several days of useless protests, his relatives sent out two parties of hunters: land hunters and sea hunters. Then everyone waited to see what would come of it.

Mouse Woman also waited to see what would come of it, though she did not stay near the village to wait. Instead, she spirited her invisible self along the trails with the land hunters. (After all, as her fellow narnauks so often reminded her, the sea was none of her business.) IF these humans had gone on such a foolish quest, they might need a little help. And she would help them because the sooner they saw the foolishness of their young chief's idea, the better it would be for everybody; for then he would get on with finding a proper wife. In fact, she decided, she would slip dreams into the hunters' sleep to guide them to the Robin Village.

For days and days the hunters searched along the trails, but nowhere did they meet a supernatural woman. The wind whipping the golden leaves from the trees along the rivers reminded them that winter was coming, with its ice and snow. So they hurried on. They were weary and discouraged when they finally came upon a large plain by a river up in the mountains. And there, on the plain, was a handsome village where everyone seemed to be young and cheery, where everyone seemed to be singing like a bird.

"This is a supernatural village," the hunters whispered to one another. Their alert eyes saw that the houses were carved and painted with unfamiliar totems. Instead of Bear and Eagle and Frog and Wolf and Killer Whale, there were stylized images of birds and flowers. They approached with thumping hearts.

At their approach, one of the cheery young people ran chirping to the biggest house to alert the head chief. Minutes later, he came to them with an invitation to enter.

Swallowing their fear of the unknown, the hunters went into the chief's house. Inside, all was as cheery as it had been outside. A fire blazed in the center, throwing an oddly sunny light on screens and houseposts. A sweetness hung in the air, as though it were springtime when the cottonwoods were leafing along the rivers. And the people inside, as young as the people outside, were singing like birds.

"Come and sit with me, dear hunters!" the chief twittered from his great painted seat at the rear of the fire; for even *his* voice had the strange chirpiness.

"Bring food for my guests!" he sang out as the men were seating themselves on the mats he had indicated.

No sooner had they seated themselves than the young hunter farthest from the chief felt something poke his leg. When he glanced down, there stood the tiniest of tiny grandmothers.

"Mouse Woman!" he whispered, glancing anxiously about to be sure no one else saw her.

"Do you know whose village this is?" she demanded in small but imperious squeaks.

"No," the young hunter whispered.

"This is the village of Chief Robin, who will let you have his beautiful daughter for your chief's wife IF you promise to take good care of her." Without another squeak, Mouse Woman vanished—even before the young hunter could stir himself to find wool for her ravelly little fingers.

He waited his chance to speak to the chief hunter. "We have found Robin Woman," he whispered while they were eating astonishingly fresh salmon and astonishingly fresh berries. He repeated what Mouse Woman had told him.

The chief hunter waited for the proper moment to speak to his host. When it came he said, "Great Chief! We have come from faraway to visit you because we have heard of your greatness and your wealth. Our young chief has sent us because he wishes to marry your beautiful daughter. He and his people will honor her and love her and make her the greatest of all the Tsimshian chieftainesses."

After consultation with the chief, the speaker took the carved talking stick in his hands; he pounded it four times on the floor; and he said, "Friends! Tomorrow the chief will invite his relatives to discuss the marriage. In two days we will let you know their answer."

When the two days had passed, Chief Robin himself spoke to the young chief's messengers. "Friends!" he said, "my wise men and all my people have decided that you may take my daughter to be your young chief's wife. We have your promise that you will take good care of her; we know you will honor that promise. And when the worst of the winter comes, let your young chief send two large canoes to me that I may fill them with provisions for his people. My wise men and all my people have decided that, for now, we will send the princess to her husband almost empty handed. We will send only two small root-baskets, one filled with fresh meat and fat, one filled with fresh berries. That is all we will send."

"Great Chief!" the chief hunter graciously protested, "you will send happiness to our chief and his people."

Yet it seemed strange that so great and wealthy a chief should send his only daughter to her marriage without relatives or attendants or costly gifts. Still, supernatural beings were different; they did things differently.

The hunters started happily homeward. And with winter coming on, they were glad to have Robin Woman leading them, showing them the best way back to their own village. She sang as she walked along; and scatters of early snow melted before her as snow had always melted before the singing of robins.

IN THE MEANTIME, the sea hunters, too, were searching for a wife for their young chief. But without Mouse Woman slipping dreams into their sleep, they came upon no supernatural village.

After much paddling and much searching among the headlands and islands, they did come upon a young woman walking along a sandy beach. From a strange brightness about her, they knew she must be a supernatural woman. And though she was not as beautiful as they had hoped, she was slender and handsomely dressed; her almost shaggy brown hair was ornamented with pretty sea shells.

"The spirits have guided us to her," the chief sea hunter said. And he ordered the canoe ashore.

"I am Sawbill Duck Woman," she told them as they approached her. Her voice was hoarser than the soft voices of their own women, they noticed. But she was supernatural and she was of the sea, as some of the sawbill ducks were.

"Our young chief wants to marry you, Sawbill Duck Woman," the chief sea hunter told her. "He sent us to find you and take you to our village."

"I will go with you," she agreed at once.

She went just as she was, with no relatives and no attendants and no gifts at all for the young chief and his people.

IT WAS the sea hunters who arrived first back at the village. And the people welcomed Sawbill Duck Woman with awed respect; for she was a supernatural being. They tended her carefully, feeding her the fish she liked. And as they waited for the return of the land hunters, they started preparations for a marriage feast worthy of their famous young chief and the two supernatural beings he would marry.

Then the land hunters returned with beautiful Robin Woman. As she came into the village, a cheeriness seemed to come with her. And when the women uncovered the two small root baskets to take out the food she had brought, they were filled with wonderment. For the more food they took out, the more food there was still to take out.

Only Sawbill Duck Woman watched the proceedings with unhappy eyes. For she had brought nothing with her.

The marriage feast was splendid, with chiefs and their head men and women gathered in from many villages. Everyone was enchanted with lovely, cheery Robin Woman.

Only Sawbill Duck Woman watched her with sad eyes. She saw the delight in her husband's eyes as he looked at his other wife. And as the days passed, her eyes grew more and more sad. Though the young chief treated her kindly, clearly he loved Robin Woman better. And seeing this, his people too showed their favoritism. While they were careful to serve Sawbill Duck Woman's fish with kindness and respect, they clearly delighted in Robin Woman's delight in the many foods they prepared for her. Ignoring the frowns of the anxious sea hunters, they murmured that Sawbill Duck Woman's voice *was* strangely hoarse and sad, while Robin Woman's voice was as sweet and cheery as the voices of birds in springtime.

Winter came. A long, cold, bitter winter. Food became scarce in the big cedar houses.

"My dear!" Robin Woman chirped to her anxious husband. "My father asked that you send two large canoes for provisions when the worst of the winter came."

"Canoes!" the young chief protested. What canoes could travel on a frozen river? Only near the mouth of the river was the water open enough for canoes.

"Canoes!" Robin Woman chirped. "I will go with them."

Still anxious about the ice, the young chief sent two great cedar canoes up the river. Robin Woman stood in the bow of the leading canoe. When they reached the ice, she sang as cheerily as the robins sang in springtime; and the ice melted before her, as ice had always melted before the singing of robins in springtime. She led the canoemen right to her father's village. And there, to their astonishment, they were fed on fresh salmon and fresh meat and fresh, juicy berries.

"It's always summer on one side of my father's house," Robin Woman explained, "and winter on the other." She opened a door to show them birds singing in leafy trees and hummingbirds darting about among flowers.

"I have come for the provisions," she told her father.

At once Chief Robin sent his people out to the summer side of his house to get fresh salmon and fresh meat and fresh, juicy berries. And when the canoes were filled, the canoemen paddled down river. As before, Robin Woman sang in the bow of the leading canoe, melting the ice before her.

There was joy and wonderment in the village when the canoes arrived. Fresh fish in midwinter! Fresh meat! And fresh, juicy berries! All were loud in their praise of the lovely young wife who had saved them from hunger.

The handsome young chief was delighted. Now, not only could he feed his hungry people; he could invite chiefs from other villages. He could feast them and send them home with food for *their* hungry people, raising his own prestige all along the coast. For generosity was the great virtue.

Only Mouse Woman noticed that Sawbill Duck Woman looked on with unhappy eyes. Only the invisible little busybody saw the neglected wife slip out of the house later that evening.

TAKING ON her bird form, Sawbill Duck Woman flew to *her* father's village.

Her father looked at her anxiously; for clearly she was unhappy.

"I am shamed in my husband's village," she told him. "I have brought nothing to his hungry people, while his other wife has brought two great canoeloads of provisions from her father."

Chief Sawbill Duck assembled the whole tribe and told them about it. "My daughter has been shamed before her husband's people," he told them.

"Then let us also send provisions," the wise men said. And all the people agreed.

The very next day their sea hunters went out on the water. They brought back whales, sea lions, seals, halibut and many other kinds of fish. They carved the whale blubber, the sea lion blubber, and the seal blubber; they prepared the fish. Then they filled two great canoes with this rich food of the sea. Finally, they tied the two canoes together and laid a ceremonial plank across them. And on this plank Sawbill Duck Woman seated herself. She would go back to her husband's village in a style befitting the supernatural wife of a famous young chief. A wistful hope began to brighten her sad eyes.

On their way to the village, the canoemen rested on an island. And there, hanging on a rock, was an enormous pile of mussels.

"We'll take them, too!" Sawbill Duck Woman said. For she wished to arrive at the village with as much food as possible.

"Where can we put them?" the canoemen protested. Mussels were of little account compared with the rich sea food they were taking. "Where can we put them?"

"On top of the food boxes and beside me on the plank," she happily told them.

When the canoemen had done this, they paddled on to the village, nearing it as the invited chiefs from other villages were enjoying the feast provided by Robin Woman.

A youth on the beach saw the canoes and raced in to tell the chief that his other wife was coming with two big canoes. "Two big canoes full of something!" he cried out in excitement.

"Full of what?" the chief asked him; and the sea hunters of the village raised expectant eyes. "Go and see what my other wife has brought to feast my guests!" His chest swelled with pride; for it was a very fine thing to have *two* supernatural wives bringing rich food to his village in the worst of the winter. *His* generosity to his hungry neighbors would be told up and down the coast, he thought, as he waited for word of what Sawbill Duck Woman had brought. No doubt it would be whale blubber and sea lion blubber and seal blubber, the richest of sea foods.

"What did she bring home with her?" he asked as soon as the youth had raced back into the house again.

"Uh . . . mussels," the youth admitted. And there was laughter, quickly and discreetly smothered.

"Mussels?" the chief cried out in indignation. "What kind of food is that for the chiefs of the Tsimshian tribes?" He turned a shamed face away from his guests. Was his other wife trying to make him look ridiculous?

"Go down to the canoes and capsize them!" he ordered his young men. So angry was he that he failed to catch Robin Woman's startled gasp; he failed to heed the anxious protests of his alarmed sea hunters.

Young land hunters raced down the beach.

But!

When they had rudely upset the great canoes, there was whale blubbler floating on the water, and sea lion blubber and seal blubber! They saw fish, too, floating on the water. So they raced back to tell the chief, leaving only invisible Mouse Woman to see Sawbill Duck Woman swim sadly away from the wreckage of her gifts.

Only the tiny narnauk watched as the humiliated wife and her paddlers shifted to the shape of sawbill ducks and flew out to sea, skimming so low over the water that their tails were awash; their ash-gray wings almost touched the water.

Sawbill Duck Woman had gone home to her father.

"WHALE BLUBBER!" the startled young chief gasped when his young men had reported to him. "Sea lion blubber!" The richest of food from the sea. "Gather it quickly and bring it in!"

Still unaware of the troubled glances of Robin Woman and the alarmed gasps of his sea hunters, he turned to his attendants. "The chiefs of the Tsimshian tribes will feast now on the richest of sea foods! They will take the richest of sea foods, too, home to their hungry people!" And now his chest swelled once more. For *his* generosity to his hungry neighbors would indeed be told up and down the coast.

But the young men raced back in from the beach with terrible tidings. "The blubber has turned into rocks and boulders!" they cried out in dismay.

"Rocks and boulders!" the young chief said, aghast at this loss of rich food and even more aghast at being made to look ridiculous. "Where is Sawbill Duck Woman?"

The answer came in small but imperious squeaks. "She has gone where any shamed wife would go," Mouse Woman told him, appearing suddenly out of thin air. "She has gone home to her father."

"Mouse Woman!" people gasped. "Grandmother!" they said again, with anxious awe. For

Mouse Woman was a narnauk; and clearly she was angry over their treatment of the chief's other wife.

Then it was Robin Woman who spoke; and her voice was no longer cheery. "I, too, am shamed by what has happened. I, too, will go home to my father." She slipped to the door so swiftly that only a few children watched in wonderment as she flew off, like a robin.

She had left the village where the cold hardness of her husband's heart had not melted before her singing.

He had lost both his wives.

"And so he should!" Mouse Woman squeaked to herself as she started homeward. Anyone so muddleheaded as, first, to want to marry two supernatural women and, then, to fail in respect for the dignity of one of them needed to learn a thing or two.

One of the things he would learn was that he had made himself ridiculous. For the story of *his* generosity would indeed be told up and down the coast.

Mouse Woman's perverse delight in that almost made up for the fact that there had been no wool at all in it for her ravelly little fingers.

The Rumor

THERE WAS A RUMOR that the first muddlehead Mouse Woman had ever dealt with was a greedy but none-too-bright narnauk called Big-Raven. And the story said that she had confronted him with her children.

Of course it was only a rumor. For who could think that Mouse Woman had ever been anything but the spirited, imperious little busybody they all called Grandmother? Who could think that she had ever been a young mother with her own Mouse Children keeping her so busy that she had no time to go out watching for other young people who had been tricked into trouble?

"Still, it might be true," people said to one another. After all, any grandmother must have been young at some time or other.

According to the rumor, her encounter with Big-Raven had happened in the time of very, very, very long before. Long before some of the real people had migrated southward along the coast to build their handsome totem pole villages. Long before Mouse Woman herself had moved southward into the Place of Supernatural Beings to watch the world with her big, busy mouse eyes.

It had happened—if indeed it had happened!—when Mouse Woman was still living with her Mouse People relatives far to the north of the Place.

One day, according to the rumor, her children were playing on the beach. And as always when they played on the beach, they were alert for shellfish they might take home to their mother to cook. For the family was very, very fond of nibbling on seafood.

Suddenly one of the children squealed with excitement. And the others came running to see what she had found.

Soon they were all squealing and squeaking with excitement. For what she had found was a small ringed seal that had been washed up on the beach and left there by the tide.

Then one of the boys gave a squeak of alarm. And everyone looked around to see what had alarmed him.

"Big-Raven!" several of them gasped. For Big-Raven was the greediest being in the village. Also, he was so big that he could take the seal away from them, and he was so tricky that he could easily convince everyone that *he* had found it.

They had to hide the seal from his greedy eyes. So they threw seaweed over it. Then they all scrambled over the seal as if they were playing on a rock. "Let's stay here on the rock and play talking games!" one of them called out, loud enough for Big-Raven to hear him.

But Big-Raven's eyes were sharp. He knew there was no rock on that spot. He knew the Mouse Children were hiding *food* from him. So, being tricky as well as greedy, he sat down on a driftlog near the beached seal. And he began to sound very unhappy.

"What can I do?" he moaned, scratching his head and then shaking his hands as if the scratching had hurt them. "What can I do? My hair is full of twigs and sand and bugs, and I can't get them out because my hands hurt. I hurt them moving and cutting up the PILES OF WHALE MEAT that are crowding me out of my house." Again he tried to run his fingers through his huge mop of tangled hair. And again he shook his hands as if the scratching had hurt them.

The Mouse Children watched him with unhappy eyes. Big-Raven was clearly in pain.

"I wonder why he didn't get his wife to clean his hair," one of the Mouse Children said.

"Oh, probably she's too busy with the whale meat," another answered. For they were very trusting little beings.

Suddenly he turned to them. "If only you could

help me!" he groaned, holding out his poor hands to them. "But why should you help me when you just want to sit on that rock and play talking games?" He looked ready to cry with the pain of it all.

The Mouse Children looked at one another.

"He is in pain," one of them whispered.

"And he has lots of food at home," another of them noted.

"I . . . suppose . . . we could help him," they all agreed.

So, transforming themselves into their mouse forms, they scampered over to Big-Raven; they scurried up to his huge mop of tangled hair and began to search for the twigs and the sand and the bugs that were making him so unhappy.

"I don't see any twigs," one of them squeaked.

"I don't see any bugs," another of them agreed.

"Then you'd better go away!" Big-Raven croaked. He jumped to his feet and shook his huge mop of tangled hair, tossing the trusting little Mouse People against logs and rocks and even into the sea. Then he made for the ringed seal.

Once more in their human forms, the battered little Mouse Children huddled together in a forlorn group. Big-Raven had tricked them. He had taken their food. Limping and crying, they went home to tell their mother.

Mouse Woman looked at them in dismay. "What happened to you?" she asked them.

"We found a ringed seal on the beach," they told her. "But Big-Raven took it from us." They sobbed out the whole story.

"Then we shall take it back again!" Mouse Woman announced, without a second thought for *their* size and *his* size. "We'll take it as he took it, by trickery." For that would make everything equal.

The Mouse Children began to feel better. "But what can we do?" they implored their mother, thinking of *their* size and *his* size.

"Big-Raven is big and greedy and tricky, but he is also none too bright," Mouse Woman reminded them. Her eyes were flashing with ideas. Her nose was twitching. "Fetch me some hand-wiping grass!" she ordered. "And I will work a spell on it." For of course, being a narnauk, Mouse Woman could work magical spells.

"Now can we go for *our* food?" the children asked when they had brought the grass, and their mother had started to work a spell on it.

"Not yet," she told them. "First, we will let him do our work for us." Her eyes had begun to twinkle. "We won't take back our food until Big-Raven and his wife have skinned it and cut it up and cooked it." It was only right to put him to some extra trouble when he had put them to some extra trouble. "You must keep an eye on Big-Raven's house and tell me what is happening." At least, their size—in their mouse forms—

would let them peer into his house without anyone seeing them.

"They're skinning the seal," the children reported, the first time they came back.

"Now, they're cutting it up," they said, the next time.

"Now they're cooking it," they said, the third time.

"Good!" said Mouse Woman. "Tell me when they're ready to eat it!" She began to put out little wooden buckets and woven baskets and sealskin bags to hold the seal meat.

"Now they're ready to eat it," the children finally reported.

"If they're ready to eat it," Mouse Woman said, "then they'll need to wipe their hands." She held up the basket of hand-wiping grass on which she had worked the sleeping spell. And this time she scurried off with her children.

"What a delicious smell!" she exclaimed as she marched in through the entry hole into Big-Raven's house. "And you're all ready to eat! So isn't it fortunate that my children have gathered so much hand-wiping grass that I'm giving some to my neighbors?" She offered Big-Raven the basket.

He looked at it with suspicious eyes. "Why should you give me something?" he asked. For it was well known that Mouse Woman gave something only when something was given in return. "Why should you give ME something?"

"Because you gave my children a good lesson today," she told him. As indeed he had.

Big-Raven thought that over. But his wife, who knew nothing about the trick he had played on the Mouse Children, took the basket and put some of the hand-wiping grass into her husband's mucky fingers. "Mouse Woman is giving you a good lesson in return," she told him. "You are far too careless about wiping your hands while eating." She began to wipe her own hands.

"It's very good . . . of you . . . Mouse Woman," she said, surprisingly slowly. "It's very good of you to . . ." The rest of her words were lost in a big yawn—a yawn as big as her husband's. "I think . . . we'll have . . . a little sleep before . . ." Again her words were lost in a big yawn as she moved slowly toward the sleeping platform, with her yawning husband behind her.

"Now we'll take our food," Mouse Woman told her children. And they all scampered outside for the wooden buckets and woven baskets and seal-skin bags they'd brought with them; at the same time they carted in some sharp stones. Then, while Big-Raven and his wife slept and slept and slept, the Mouse Family carried full buckets and baskets and bags one way, and empty buckets and baskets and bags the other way until all the meat had been taken.

"We won't try to take the soup," Mouse Woman told them. "But it's too bad to leave it with no bits of anything in it. Throw in the sharp stones!"

Her children delightedly splashed in some sharp stones.

"Save the sharpest ones for his boots!" their mother reminded them. And she herself dropped the sharpest stones into Big-Raven's sealskin boots.

Then they all trooped wearily home for a good feed of seal meat.

IT WAS LATE the next morning before Big-Raven and his wife woke up, ravenously hungry.

Big-Raven got up and pulled on a sealskin boot.

"O ko ko ko ko!" he yelled, dancing about in pain. "Someone has put sharp stones into my boot!"

"And into the soup!" his wife wailed, stirring it.

"Then serve the meat!" Big-Raven croaked, hurling sharp stones every which way. And as he picked up the sharp stones and hurled them every which way, his hands actually did start to hurt the way he had pretended they hurt the day before. Only, now his feet hurt too. "Serve the meat!" he thundered.

"But . . . there's no meat to serve!" his wife wailed. Every last scrap has been taken.

"Mouse Woman did this!" Big-Raven roared. "Well! I shall attend to Mouse Woman." He picked up his seal club. "I'll kill her and her children!"

Of course he knew that he couldn't actually *kill* a narnauk; but he could certainly make Mouse Woman and her children wish they hadn't stolen HIS meat, he thought as he raced off to their house.

Mouse Woman was ready for him. As soon as the children reported that he was coming, she ladled out steaming cloudberry pudding into bowls; and they all rushed out to greet their neighbor, waving the bowls so that the fragrant steam could curl up to his nose. For it was well known that cloudberry pudding was one of Big-Raven's favorite things.

"Cloudberry pudding!" they all squealed as they waved the bowls at him.

"Cloudberry pudding?" he said, his greedy eyes devouring the luscious food.

"Whatever you've come for," Mouse Woman said, "surely it can wait until you've tasted my cloudberry pudding."

"Well . . ." Big-Raven agreed, dropping his club to snatch at one of the bowls.

"I've made far too much for us," Mouse Woman told him. As indeed she had. "Eat all you want, Big-Raven!"

He did not need to be coaxed. He ate and ate and ate cloudberry pudding. And before he had time to think very clearly of anything else, Mouse Woman pushed a basket of hand-wiping grass at him. He wiped his mucky hands. Then he yawned such a big yawn that the Mouse Children cowered back from the huge cave in his face.

"Rest yourself!" Mouse Woman invited.

Soon he was sound asleep.

"Now!" Mouse Woman ordered, for she was really ready for his visit. She held out a basket of seal hairs that she had dyed red. And the children at once began to glue them on to Big-Raven's eyelids.

After some time, Big-Raven stirred. Still muddled by the sleeping spell, he opened his eyes and saw everything RED around him. "Fire!" he yelled as he leaped up and raced out of the house.

"Muddlehead!" Mouse Woman chuckled as she and her children watched him roar off toward his own house.

"The world is on fire!" he yelled to his wife. "Our house is on fire!"

"Nonsense!" his wife said. "Do you smell smoke? Do you hear flames?"

"N . . . no," he admittd. "But the world looks very odd."

"YOU look very odd," his wife countered. "What's the matter with your eyes?"

"What's the matter with my eyes?" He put a trembling hand up to them and felt a FUR of eyelashes.

"Dyed seal hairs," his wife said, yanking one off to show him. "Mouse Woman has tricked you

. . . WHY has she tricked you?" she asked. For it was well known that Mouse Woman tricked someone only when that someone had tricked her.

Big-Raven was too busy to answer. He was yanking off the dyed seal hairs and dancing about with the pain of it all. "I'll fix her!" he roared. "I'll kill her and her children!"

But his eyelids were much too sore for him to kill them at the moment. Besides, seeing his hands all red from the dye, his wife had pushed Mouse Woman's basket of hand-wiping grass at him. And he had begun to feel strangely sleepy.

It was the next morning when he woke up. "Give me something to eat!" he croaked as he felt carefully inside his sealskin boots before pulling them on.

"But there's nothing to give you," his wife said. "Remember?"

Big-Raven remembered. "I'll kill Mouse Woman and her children!" he roared as he picked up his stone hammer and raced out of the house.

Again, Mouse Woman was ready for him. As soon as the children reported that he was coming, she ladled out steaming blackberry pudding into bowls; and they all rushed out to greet their neighbor, waving the bowls so the fragrant steam would curl up to his nose. For it was well known that blackberry pudding was one of Big-Raven's favorite things.

"Blackberry pudding!" they all squealed as they

waved the bowls at him.

"Blackberry pudding?" he said; and his greedy eyes were devouring the luscious food.

"Whatever you've come for," Mouse Woman said, "surely it can wait until you've tasted my blackberry pudding."

"Well . . ." Big-Raven agreed, dropping his stone hammer to snatch at one of the bowls.

"I've made far too much for us," Mouse Woman told him. As indeed she had. "Eat all you want, Big-Raven!"

He did not need to be coaxed. He ate and ate and ate blackberry pudding. And before he had time to think very clearly of anything else, Mouse Woman pushed a basket of hand-wiping grass at him. He wiped his mucky hands. Then he yawned such a big yawn that the Mouse Children cowered back from the huge cave in his face.

"Rest yourself!" Mouse Woman invited.

Soon he was sound asleep.

"Now!" Mouse Woman ordered, for once more she was really ready for his visit. She handed out pots of paint and charcoal. And the children at once began to make splendid patterns on Big-Raven's face.

"Paint him to look like the Woman of Many Colors!" Mouse Woman reminded them. She was an awesome being who sometimes came to the stream Big-Raven would pass on his way home. It was a deep, quiet stream running into the big, turbulent river that emptied into the sea.

By the time he woke up, Big-Raven's face was hideous with blue and red and yellow and black patterns. And the Mouse Children were staring at him as if they were anxious. Which indeed they were. Especially when they glanced at his stone hammer.

"Oh dear, dear, dear, dear!" Mouse Woman exclaimed. "Do you feel well, Big-Raven?"

"Feel . . . well?" he muttered. None too bright at any time, he was now muddled by the sleeping spell as well as by all the anxious faces.

"Oh dear, dear, dear, dear!" Mouse Woman said again. "Perhaps you ate too much pudding." Which was certainly true. "Hurry! You must drink lots of water on your way home!"

"Drink . . . lots of water . . . on my way home?" he muttered, picking up his stone hammer and staggering off toward his own house.

He staggered along until he came to the stream. "Drink lots of water," he muttered, squatting down by the stream and bending over to drink as he laid down his hammer.

But! A painted face looked up at him from the still, deep, cold water.

"Woman of Many Colors!" he whispered, awestruck. She was an awesome being. And he had nothing to offer her as a sign of peace and friendship. So who knew what she might do to him? Now Big-Raven was terrified as well as muddled.

The hammer! He had his stone hammer with him. He could offer her his stone hammer. So he picked it up and leaned over to offer it to the Woman of Many Colors. And he fell in.

Big-Raven spluttered. He flailed his arms and his legs, getting away from the being he had seen in the water.

Before he knew what he was doing, he flailed himself right into the big, turbulent river. And the big, turbulent river carried him out to sea.

There, according to the rumor, he took on his raven form and disappeared for some time. And no one ever seemed to have heard of another attempt to get back at Mouse Woman and her children.

"STILL, THERE MUST have been four tricks," everyone agreed.

But that was the thing about a rumor. It wasn't sure and proper like one of the great stories they told in the feast houses, where everything happened four times.

Yet it might be true, people said. Indeed, maybe it was why Mouse Woman was always so ready to help any young people who'd been tricked into trouble.

Anyway, it had happened—if indeed it had happened!—in the time of very, very, very, very long before, when things were different.

The Princess and Copper Canoeman

"SOMETIMES I THINK I'm a little muddleheaded myself," Mouse Woman told Copper Canoeman. "Especially when I'm dealing with handsome young men."

Copper Canoeman was a very handsome young man. Though he was a supernatural being, he appeared always as a young man, never as an animal. Which made it a little more reasonable for *him* to yearn for a human princess.

"Still," the tiny Grandmother reminded him, "marriage with a human princess would not be a proper marriage." Her nose twitched, just thinking of how *im*proper it would be.

"What I have now is a proper marriage?" he challenged her. For what he had now was no marriage at all. Under pressure from one of the monsters, his family had arranged a marriage for him with Wolverine Woman, a dreadful being whose only delight was to spend her nights noisily chewing up seals, bones and all.

Because he was the dreadful being's husband, Copper Canoeman had almost stopped his own copper working to spend *his* nights catching seals to keep Wolverine Woman greedily crunching. The rest of his time he spent yearning for a beautiful young lady who would be a real wife to a lonely young man who had moved, of necessity, to a small island off the mouth of a river. After all, it was the custom for high ranking men to have more than one wife.

"Help me, Grandmother!" he pleaded.

"Help you do something improper?" Mouse Woman retorted. Yet her big busy mouse eyes lingered wistfully over his sad face. "Well," she conceded, "if I ever do see a human princess in such a desperate plight that only marriage with you could save her, I might guide her your way. But wait until I send her!"

"I will wait, Grandmother!" Joyfully he hoisted the tiny narnauk up in the air, in spite of her indignant protests. "I have a gift for you," he said, when he had put her down again.

"I should think so!" Mouse Woman squeaked. For not only did she deserve payment for agreeing to help him; she deserved recompense, also, for having had her dignity undermined. She took the wool he offered as no more than her due. And she scarcely waited until he had gone before eagerly tearing at it with her ravelly little fingers.

"Sometimes I think I'm a little muddleheaded myself," she told herself, thinking of what she had half promised. Marriage between a supernatural being and a human was most improper. "Still . . ."

Still, she began to keep a close watch on all the nearby princesses. Just in case one *should* get into such a desperate plight that only marriage with Copper Canoeman could save her.

Now, AS IT HAPPENED, there was a nearby princess who might well get into such a desperate plight. A Black Bear narnauk had his eye on her; for he, too, wanted to marry a human princess. Being too great a chief to go roaming around capturing princesses himself, he had sent his son out to do it for him. And Son-of-Black-Bear's invisible self was already hovering about, waiting. What he was waiting for was some cruel action on the part of a certain princess, some disrespect to the bears that would justify his carrying her off.

The princess, Summer Stream, was a gentle girl who would not have been cruel to a mosquito, much less to a bear. Since she loved to go berry picking with the girls who were her friends-and-attendants, she went often into the Bear People's favorite berry patch. So, Mouse Woman knew, it was only a matter of time until Son-of-Black-

Bear found an excuse to take her.

The time was not long in coming.

One day the princess went out berry picking. And since she couldn't resist following birds and butterflies, her basket was by no means full when the others were ready to go home.

Now it was a point of pride with high-ranking young people to do everything and do it well. So, since Summer Stream would never go home with a half-empty basket, her friends started slipping some of their own berries into her basket.

"Princess! Your basket is full enough now," one of the girls said. "It's time for us to go home."

Summer Stream, who had not been paying all that much attention to her berries, readily agreed. And they started down the mountain.

Even walking home along the trail, she could not keep her eyes off the birds and the butterflies. So it was that one bare foot stepped into some fresh bear dung. She slipped and fell down, spilling some of the precious berries from the basket that was held on her back by a carrying strap around her forehead.

"Oh dear!" she cried out, aghast at what had happened. "Those stupid bears!"

Her friends gasped at this disrespect to the bears. All day they had been careful to sing as they picked so that they might not offend a bear by coming upon him suddenly, unannounced. "But never mind," they comforted her as one of them cleaned her foot while the others picked up the best of the scattered berries. Again concerned for her pride, they slipped a few more of their own berries into her basket.

They had not gone much farther along the trail before her carrying strap broke. Which was strange; for her strap, made of fresh young wool, had been tested that very morning.

"Oh dear!" she cried out again. For again some of the precious berries had been spilled out.

"Never mind," her friends comforted her. And once more they picked up the best of the scattered berries and slipped a few more of their own berries into her basket.

This time Summer Stream saw them and stopped them. "At this rate, there will be no berries at all to take home to the village," she told them. "So I shall sit here and wait while you take your berries home and send someone back to help me."

Her friends protested. But the princess insisted. "Just send someone back to help me!" she ordered as she settled herself on a log where she could watch the birds and the butterflies.

Reluctantly her friends-and-attendants left her. "Someone will come very soon to help you," they promised.

In fact, someone came surprisingly soon, someone she did not recognize as a young man from her village. Perhaps her friends had met this handsome fellow on the trail, she thought. Though his voice was oddly gruff, he seemed to be a friendly stranger.

"Follow me, Princess!" he said in his oddly gruff voice when he had picked up her basket and started along the trail. "Good ripe berries!" he exclaimed, scooping up a handful and slapping them into his mouth. "Very good ripe berries!" he went on, scooping up yet another handful and slapping them, too, into his mouth. And so it went until the basket was empty.

Summer Stream was so amazed, watching him gobble up all the precious berries, that she failed to notice he was leading her along a different trail.

"No more berries!" he finally cried out in his oddly gruff voice. And with one mighty slap of his hand, he broke the basket. He tossed it off into the bushes. Then he turned to smile at her.

"Oh dear!" she gasped. It was not his treatment of her basket that had alarmed her. It was the big teeth he had bared in his stained mouth. "Oh dear!" she said again, glancing fearfully about her. "Where . . . are we going?" she asked in a frightened whisper.

"To my father's house!" he growled at her. "Come on!" He grabbed her hand and pulled her roughly along.

Sputtering protests and tripping from the pace he set with his long lumbering strides, the princess grew more and more terrified. Who was he? And where was he taking her?

At last they came to a village she had never seen before, a village up in the mountains, deep in a valley ringed by steep cliffs. They stopped before a huge cedar house decorated with Bear totems—Bear totems she had never seen before, Bear totems with such enormous teeth that she shuddered. Who was he? And where had he brought her? Trembling with terror, she waited to see what would happen next.

"Did you get what you went for?" a voice growled from somewhere inside the house.

"I got what I went for."

"Then bring her in!"

The princess blinked from the smoke as they went into the big, windowless house. Firelight flickered on houseposts that were horrifyingly like monster black bears; it showed her a huge chief sitting at the rear of the fire, a chief whose bulky head seemed to wag from side to side as his small eyes peered at her. In his fur robe, he was alarmingly like a monster bear.

"Sit by the fire, my dear!" the chief invited; and his smile bared *his* big teeth.

Summer Stream swallowed and sat down. Then, peering fearfully about, she saw many bearskins hanging along the walls. She saw bears as well as people snuffling about in the dark corners. No one was paying any attention to her. But what were they planning as they talked in gruff voices around the chief?

Suddenly, she felt something small and furry

tickle her knee. Glancing down, she saw a white mouse emerge from under her cedar bark dress. And then, there stood the tiniest of tiny grandmothers.

"Mouse Woman!" she gasped in a thankful whisper. For it was well known that Mouse Woman was a friend to young people who'd been tricked into trouble.

"Have you any wool?" the tiny narnauk demanded in small but imperious squeaks.

"Yes, Grandmother!" Summer Stream whispered. Swiftly she tore one of the woolen fringes from her belt. For it was also well known that Mouse Woman demanded payment for her help, to keep everything equal.

"Do you know who has taken you?" the tiny narnauk asked as her ravelly little fingers began tearing at the wool.

"No."

"The Black Bear People. Their chief plans to marry you. But I will help you. First, do not eat the berries and crabapples they will offer you, for the crabapples are not real crabapples; they are the eyes of dead people. And they would turn *you* into what *they* are. Later, you may eat the salmon."

At that moment, the group around the chief turned toward her. But Mouse Woman had vanished into thin air.

"Feed my bride!" the chief growled.

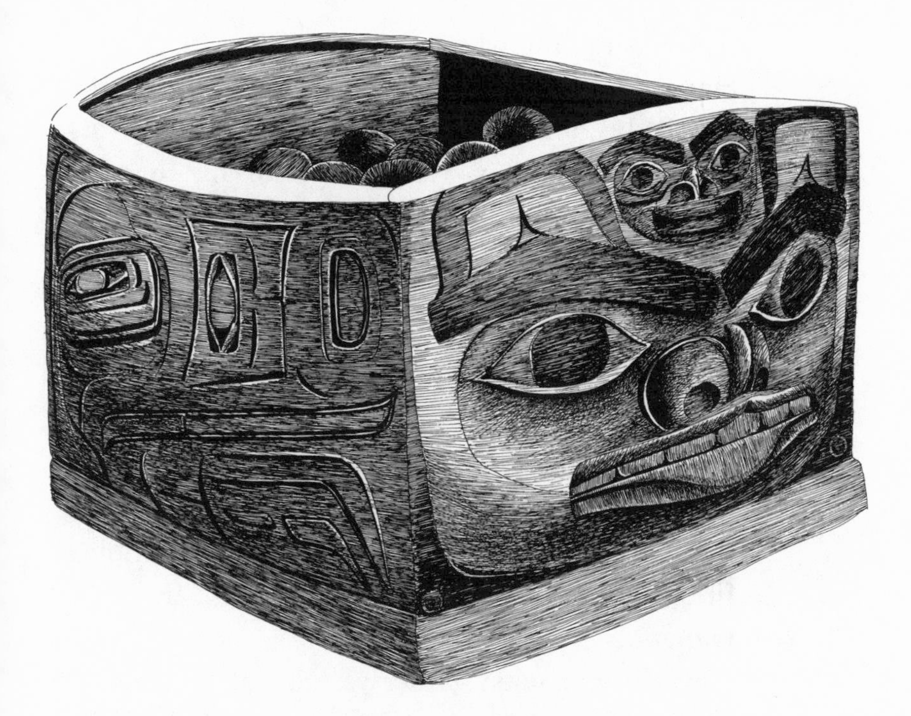

At once a slave brought a wooden bowl filled with berries and crabapples. When the princess refused this, the chief glared at her. But another slave brought another bowl, this time a bowl of salmon.

While she was nibbling at a small piece, she noticed that two small women were watching her with hostile little black eyes. They watched her again as she was shown to a sleeping platform.

The next day it was the same two small women who took her out to gather wood for the fire. And the princess, who knew well how to gather firewood, was careful to choose good dry pieces.

It was raining when she returned to Black Bear House. And when her wood was thrown on the fire, it did not seem to burn well. When Son-of-Black-Bear came in, wet, and shook his fur robe over the fire, the scattered drops of water put the fire out.

The two small women glared at her, as if it were her fault. What had she done wrong?

Later, when she was on her sleeping platform, Summer Stream felt something small and furry tickle her knee. And there, once more, was Mouse woman.

At once the princess pulled the other woolen fringe from her belt and gave it to the tiny narnauk.

"Here you must gather wood that is green or watersoaked," Mouse Woman advised. "The women are the chief's sisters, his spies. They will watch you constantly to see that you don't escape. But I will help you to escape when the time comes."

"Yes, Grandmother!" Summer Stream whispered, hoping that the time would come soon. For, as time went on, the chief seemed more and more terrifying; his teeth seemed bigger and bigger.

The next day, when the two small women again took her out to gather firewood, she was careful to find pieces that had been waterlogged, though they were horribly heavy to carry. And this time, when Son-of-Black-Bear shook his wet fur robe over the fire, the scattered drops of water made it blaze up.

That night she could scarcely sleep, waiting for the tiny narnauk. She had pulled much wool from her belt before she again felt the small furry tickle.

"Tomorrow you will escape from the sisters," Mouse Woman told her as she tore at the wool with her ravelly little fingers. "You must insist on searching for wetter and wetter wood until you come to a wide stump by the river. Then you must insist on helping the sisters to adjust the packs on their backs. And to do this, you must put their wood packs on the stump; and while they have their backs to one another, across the stump, you must tie them together. Your long belt will be strong enough to hold them. If you don't keep tearing it to pieces!" she added tartly.

"Yes, Grandmother."

"When you escape, you must run downstream until you come to the mouth of the river and see a young man in a copper canoe. Ask him to help you, even if you have to offer to marry him."

"Marry him?" the princess gasped.

"Unless you prefer to marry Chief Black Bear. Copper Canoeman is a kind man."

"Yes . . . Grandmother," Summer Stream whispered, between swallows. But she found she was whispering to thin air. Mouse Woman had vanished.

NEXT MORNING, the princess went willingly with the sisters to gather firewood. But to their annoyance, she simply could not find any wet enough to suit her. Only when she saw a wide stump by the river, did she begin to find wood she wanted.

"Oh, let me help you adjust your packs!" she said to the sisters, who still watched her with their hostile little black eyes. "I'm very good at adjusting packs." Without waiting for their consent, she heaved their heavy packs up onto the stump. "If you'll stand here, and here, I can do it very quickly."

Suspecting nothing, the sisters followed their packs to the stump and stood waiting, with their backs to one another.

Summer Stream, chattering away about the packs as she worked, tied the sisters to one another, across the stump. Then she fled downstream.

Growling with rage, the two small women tried to follow her: But they were tied securely together by the long woolen belt. Their enraged growls reached the girl's ears as she fled along the riverbank, scrambling over driftwood and tearing her dress on sharp snags.

She had still not reached the mouth of the river when she heard a different enraged growling, coming from somewhere far behind her.

Son-of-Black-Bear!

In rising panic, she frantically scrambled over driftwood, tearing her dress to shreds. Now she could hear driftwood cracking and crashing behind her, and dislodged rocks rolling. Terrifying growls were growing louder and louder.

Then she saw the mouth of the river; she saw a copper canoe glinting out on the water.

"Copper Canoeman!" she cried out. But he did not seem to hear her.

The cracking and crashing and rolling of rocks were very close now. The growls were horrifying.

"Copper Canoeman!" she shrieked. "Help me! Help me! My father will pay you well to help me!"

Still he did not seem to hear her. And the terrifying noises were almost on her.

"Help me!" she shrieked again. "I will marry you if you help me!"

Now he did hear. He touched a copper paddle to the gunwhale. And with a wonderful DONG, the copper canoe shot toward her. And just as Son-of-Black-Bear was grabbing for her, she took the young canoeman's hand and stepped into the canoe. With another DONG, the canoe shot out into deep water, leaving the enraged narnauk splashing and flailing and growling by the riverbank.

The princess had escaped.

"Copper Canoeman!" she gasped gratefully. And now she saw that he was a very handsome young man. His smile warmed her heart. Clearly, as Mouse Woman had said, he was a kind man. But as clearly, he was a narnauk. And she had promised to marry him.

"Princess, I will take you to my island," he told her. And with another DONG, the copper canoe shot out to sea, out to a remote island.

"I already have one wife," he told her as the canoe grated on the beach. "A strange woman. So you must do nothing to annoy her!" He looked anxiously at Summer Stream before he went on to describe the strangeness. "She will cook for us, but she will not eat with us. . . . Princess, no matter what strange noises you hear at night, while I am away, you must not give way to curiosity. You must not look into her part of the house!"

"I will not look into her part of the house," the princess promised. And she felt panic rising again. What strange noises would she hear? And what would happen if she did look?

A woman came down to the beach to meet them. A strange, hairy woman whose eyes were quick and cunning, whose fingers made the girl think of an animal's claws. Yet she welcomed Summer Stream as a sister before she turned, almost greedily, to pick up the seals the young man had in his canoe. With astonishing strength, she began to carry them, one by one, to the house.

"Beware of her!" Copper Canoeman warned. "Especially at night! No matter what you hear, you must not peer into her part of the house. For she is a terrible being who could eat your soul."

The girl shuddered. What was she going to hear? And what would the woman be doing to make such a noise? She had escaped. But what had she escaped to?

The woman fed them good cooked seal, but she did not eat with them. When she had fed them, she disappeared into her part of the house—a part where the firelight did not reach. No sounds came from her.

The girl felt her panic rising. Only when she looked at Copper Canoeman did she feel safe again. For truly he was a handsome young man, and a kind one. When night came, he showed her to her sleeping platform. Then he went off to catch seals.

Now she was alone with the terrible being who could eat her soul. She was alone with the terrifyingly mysterious Being on a remote, lonely island. She longed for her home and her loving, guarding family. She longed for a small furry tickle. But Mouse Woman did not appear.

Suddenly, she was roused from a restless sleep by a horrible, cracking, grinding noise, as if someone were crushing bones. She pulled her blanket up over her ears. But the noise still came to her. What was the woman doing?

Finally, she went to sleep again. And when she

woke once more, she heard only voices and the familiar sounds of cooking.

Again the woman gave her good cooked seal meat, though the princess longed for salmon and berries to eat by the blazing fire in her father's house.

On the following night, the same things happened. The woman disappeared into her own part of the house. Copper Canoeman went out to catch seals. And Summer Stream crept fearfully to her sleeping platform, waiting for the dreadful noises. Which were not long in starting—the horrible, cracking, grinding noises, as if someone were crushing bones. Again she pulled her blanket up over her ears. But the noises still came to her. What was the woman doing?

It was at dawn, on the fourth night, when she could no longer smother her curiosity. Hugging her blanket around her, she crept from her sleeping platform toward the forbidden part of the house, toward the horrible, cracking, grinding noises. She peered fearfully through a hole in the blanket.

The woman was devouring raw seals, bones and all, greedily crushing them with her terrible teeth.

The princess gasped.

The woman glanced up. Then she choked on a bone and writhed in agony until she had cleared her throat.

By this time, Summer Stream was back in her bed. Trembling with terror, she heard the dreadful being's approach. Then, mercifully, the world was blotted out.

As Copper Canoeman had warned, the glutton had eaten her soul. And with her spirit self gone, Summer Stream's body lay as though dead.

OUT AT SEA, Copper Canoeman sensed the danger to the beautiful princess he intended to marry. He touched his copper paddle to the gunwale of his copper canoe. And with a DONG, the canoe shot through the waters, home to his island.

Wolverine Woman was waiting on the beach.

"Where is Summer Stream?" he asked her.

"Oh, my dear sister is still asleep," she told him before she turned, almost greedily, to pick up the seals in his canoe.

Knowing that she lied, Copper Canoeman raced to where the princess was lying. Then he raced out again. "You have killed her!" he cried out. And seizing his copper seal club, he hurled it at the terrible being.

The club knocked her head off. And before it could attach itself once more to the being's body, he rubbed the severed neck with a poison he had made of devil's club and skunk cabbage. Then he tore Wolverine Woman's heart out. He waved it four times over the girl's motionless body.

Summer Stream stirred on her sleeping platform. She opened her eyes, blinked, and glanced about her. She saw the young man with the bleeding heart in his hand.

"What . . . happened?" she whispered, shrinking back from the bleeding heart.

"What will never happen to you again," he said.

"You've killed her!" the girl gasped.

"No, I've not killed her. Such beings as she cannot be killed. They can only be transformed."

To work the transformation, he dried the heart, pulverized it, and scattered it to the winds. The winds carried it to the land, where it took life again in many small furry bodies. Wolverine Woman's body was dead and was carried off by her relatives. But her gluttony and her cunning lived on in tribes of wolverines.

Now Copper Canoeman married Summer Stream. And for a time, they were happy together. Then she began to long for her old home, for her old loving family. She began to yearn for the old berry patches and the old, familiar gatherings in the feast houses.

When her son was born, she longed to show him to her relatives. And though her husband trained him in marvelous copper working, she yearned to have him trained as the boys in her family had always been trained.

At last Copper Canoeman sadly sent her back to her own people with a supernatural son who was destined to become a famous and wealthy copperworker.

"SOMETIMES I THINK I'm a muddlehead myself," Mouse Woman told Copper Canoeman when he was once more a lonely young man yearning for a beautiful wife. "I should never have helped you to have an *im*proper marriage."

Asdilda and Omen

ONCE IN THE DAYS of very long ago, on the big offshore islands of the Haida people, there was a chief who had a wife and two children, Asdilda and Omen. Asdilda was growing into a willful, arrogant youth, while his sister Omen was becoming a lovely young lady; for *she* was not being spoiled by her parents.

"Muddleheads!" Mouse Woman squeaked every time she thought of the parents. They were foolishly indulgent with their son. And the tiny narnauk knew that, sooner or later, a spoiled boy brought trouble on his family.

In Asdilda's case, she thought, the trouble might well start with a hat.

As the highest-ranking prince in his group of Eagles, Asdilda had already been given the great Cormorant Hat that went with the great name he wore. Covered with the skins of cormorants and decorated with irridescent abalone shell and with a frog with copper eyes, the Cormorant Hat was an ancient tradition with the Eagle Clan. It should have been worn only on ceremonial occasions. But the foolish parents turned a blind eye when Asdilda wore it as an ordinary canoe hat.

"Muddleheads!" Mouse Woman squeaked. For not only was this treatment of the hat disrespectful to the many great chiefs who had worn it before him; it was disrespectful also to the supernatural being it had honored in the first place—the mountain spirit known sometimes as Frog Woman and sometimes as Volcano Woman. She had the power to send flaming streams of lava down over those who had offended her; and the parents should have thought of that. Besides, the Hat was too big for the boy.

Mouse Woman watched to see what would happen.

One day Asdilda called together the four high-ranking Eagle youths who were his friends-and-attendants. "We're going fishing for trout," he said. And he swaggered off to his canoe, wearing the Cormorant Hat.

It was springtime. The sun was turning the leafing cottonwoods into green-gold surges of scent all along the river that ran into the sea near the village. But the prince thought only of the trout he would catch—the big trout that would gladly offer themselves to the wearer of the hat.

They paddled up river until they reached the trout pool where they camped every spring. Evening was coming on, and as the prince looked down into the clear water, he saw many trout lurking under the canoe. But they were all too small to be worthy of a great prince's efforts. So he sat there, sulking, while his friends caught enough fish for supper.

"They're so small!" Asdilda exclaimed, looking at the catch with lordly disdain.

Then a big trout appeared.

Asdilda leaped up and lunged with his spear. But the Cormorant Hat fell down over his eyes, spoiling his aim. The trout got away. And the prince stamped an angry foot, rocking the canoe.

He had no sooner put the hat on again than another big trout appeared. Again, he started to spear it. Again, the hat fell down over his eyes, spoiling his aim. Again, the trout got away. It was all the hat's fault, Asdilda thought as he yanked it down on his head once more. It was all the hat's fault.

When this had happened four times, Asdilda grabbed the offending hat, furiously tore it to pieces and threw the pieces into the water. Then he sat scowling at the pool while his young steersman—aghast at this treatment of the ancient hat!—fished the pieces out with a long pole. For the hat was a valuable crest, treasured by all the Eagles.

"We'll camp now!" the prince said.

His attendants quickly made camp at the foot of the big spruce tree where they camped every spring. They built a fire. And while the others roasted the many small trout, the steersman gathered skunk cabbage leaves to serve as platters.

The boys placed the roasted trout on the leaves. They gave the biggest leaf to Asdilda. But just as he reached for his food, a frog jumped onto it. And though he shouted at it and motioned it away, it simply sat there—on HIS food!—staring at him with its big bulging eyes. So he grabbed it by the legs and hurled it into the fire.

The steersman gasped in dismay. But the other boys laughed; for, following the lead of their royal comrade, they too had become disdainful of creatures.

The frog jumped out of the fire.

The angry prince caught it and hurled it back in. And the steersman did not dare to stop him.

The frog jumped out yet again.

And yet again the prince caught it and hurled it back in. Yet again his foolish friends laughed.

The fourth time he threw it into the fire, the furious prince grabbed a pronged stick and held the frog in the fire until it burst.

Three of his friends laughed; but the eyes of the young steersman were troubled. Something was sure to happen after this bad treatment of a creature.

Later, in the dark of the night, he seemed to

hear a distant wailing. He seemed to hear a woman's voice calling, "My son! My son! Who was burned in the fire!"

Perhaps it was only a dream, he thought, when morning brought the cheerful chirping of the birds. Yet he was still troubled. Something was going to happen.

"We're going home at once," the prince told his friends as soon as he had opened his eyes. And though the other boys had expected to spend the usual several days at their favorite trout pool, they did not dare to protest. They simply gave Asdilda leftover trout to eat while they broke camp and launched the canoe. Then they paddled downriver.

They had not gone far when a young woman hailed them from a river beach. "My dears!" she called out, "please take me along with you!"

The steersman caught his breath. For there was a sadness in the lady's voice, and her face was touched with charcoal, the sign of mourning.

Asdilda, seeing nothing of her sadness, ordered the canoe ashore. He leaped out as soon as it had touched the beach, flinging out his arms to embrace the beautiful young lady.

His arms closed on thin air. Only a frog jumped away from him.

"A frog!" The steersman swallowed.

Alarmed by the strange happening, the other attendants trembled.

But Asdilda only scowled and ordered them to paddle on.

Three times this strange thing happened. Three times a beautiful young woman hailed them from a river beach. Three times the prince leaped out to embrace her. Three times his arms closed on thin air. And three times only a frog jumped away from him.

Each time a frog! Each time the steersman swallowed and the other attendants trembled. But each time the prince only scowled and ordered them to paddle on.

When a beautiful young lady hailed them from a river beach for a fourth time, Asdilda called back, "No! You will only vanish away from me!" He ordered his friends to paddle on.

As they went on, the youths heard her call out, "Listen to what I say to you! Listen! When you arrive at that next point, your prince will fall dead. At the next point, another of you will die. Then another. And another. Only your steersman will be alive when you reach the village. And he too will die as soon as he has told what has happened." She moved off, wailing, "My son! My son! Who was burned in the fire!"

"Frog Woman!" the steersman said in an awed whisper. "The mountain spirit who is also Volcano Woman!"

"My son! My son! Who was burned in the fire!" The wailing came to them from farther and farther away. "My son! My son! Who was burned in the fire!"

"Pay no attention to her!" the prince ordered. "Just go on!"

They went on. Indeed, they seemed unable now to do anything except go on. And when they reached the next point, the prince fell dead. At the next point, one of his companions fell dead. Then another. And another. As the woman had predicted, only the steersman was alive when the canoe reached the village.

"What happened?" the people of the village cried out, rushing to the beach. They saw the four motionless figures lying in the canoe. "They are dead," people murmured. And a wailing started among the women.

"What happened?" people insisted.

The young steersman opened his mouth to tell them. Then he closed it. For as soon as he had told them, he too would fall dead. He raced into the house of Asdilda's father. And the crowd followed him in.

"What happened?" they kept demanding.

Standing by the fire, the youth faced the people of the village. He would die if he told them. Yet only by telling them would they know what happened to those who forgot their proper respect for the world around them, the world of creatures and Spirit Beings.

Sadly he told them what had happened. Then,

there before their eyes, the young steersman fell dead.

"Frog Woman!" people gasped to one another as they streamed out of the house. And a great wailing started—a wailing for what had already happened and for what might still happen. For Frog Woman was also Volcano Woman. Dread filled the many eyes that looked at the mountain behind the village.

The Eagle Princess Omen wailed with the wailing women. For she had loved her willful, arrogant brother; his friends had been brothers to her. Day after day, she wandered mournfully around the village.

"I had a dream," an old woman told the people one morning. And her eyes were full of dread as she glanced at the mountain. Yet she did not tell them her dream.

"You must hide your daughter away!" she told Omen's parents.

The rumor raced through the village. The Eagle Princess was to be hidden away. Everyone knew that a princess was hidden away only when there was a terrible menace to the people whose royal bloodline she carried, only when there was need to insure that *she* would survive a catastrophe to bear sons and daughters entitled to wear the Clan's great names and the great personal crests that went with them. For only *she* could insure the survival of the Clan's prestige along the coast.

"Hide the princess!" people gasped to one another. Clearly, something dreadful was going to happen.

"Hide the great coppers and the ancient regalia and crests with her!" the old woman instructed. "And the costly sea otter robes and the elk skins!"

Clearly the village was to be wiped out.

Stunned by the loss of his son, and alarmed by further menace, the chief ordered his men to enlarge the secret chamber under the house . . . to line it with the great coppers . . . and to store it with the wealth boxes that held the ancient regalia and crests of the Eagles *and* the Ravens; for he himself was a Raven. Fortunately for the Raven Clan, its princess was living in another village.

At last all was ready. Omen was hidden away in the chamber under the house, with food and water. The chamber was covered with planks and blankets, and then with earth; the air shaft was protected. Now, whatever happened to the people who had incurred the wrath of the mountain spirit, the future of Eagle pride was insured. Eagles might die. But the Eagle Clan went on forever.

And now that *her* obligation to the future had been met, the old woman told them her dream.

"I saw in my dream that fire fell on the village," she told them. "I saw it on the mountain."

Even as she spoke, fire belched from the mountain; and as it began to flow down the mountain like flaming oil, a firebrand fell on one of the big cedar houses. The house burst into flame. Then another house burst into flame. And another. Like burning oil, fire flamed even on the water. And there was no escape for the people who had forgotten their respect for the world around them, the world of creatures and spirit beings. They were burned with their village.

WHEN THE DREADFUL SCREAMS and the terrifying noises of the fire had turned into an even more terrifying silence, the weeping princess thought she heard the voice of an old woman wailing, "I gather the bones of my dear ones, my dear ones!" Yet when she had pushed off a corner of her roof and peered out, she saw only a desolate, smouldering village. She heard only a faraway wailing comming from the mountain. A woman's voice seemed to be wailing, "My son! My son! Who was burned in the fire!"

Almost blinded by her tears, the girl peered through falling ash toward the mountain. And she saw a strangely shining chieftainess coming toward the smouldering ruins, singing her mourning song. She wore a large green hat with Frog totems; she carried a cane with a live frog at the top and a live frog at the bottom. "Frog Woman!" the girl whispered.

"My son! My son! Who was burned in the fire!"

the woman kept wailing as she wandered through the burned village. Then she vanished into thin air.

The princess made her tearful way out of the pit, out into the desolate, smouldering, ash-shrouded ruins of a once happy village. Only she had survived. Scarcely knowing what she did, she crept back into the pit.

What could she do?

Where could she go?

Stunned by the enormity of her loss, and moving almost as in a dream, Omen took a sea otter robe and a chief's fringed dancing blanket out of one of the wealth chests. She took a pouch of food. Then she climbed up out of the chamber and carefully covered it up again to keep its treasures safe. A mourning song came to her lips:

When went to spear fish my dear prince, alas!
When went to spear fish my dear prince, alas!
Then fell the Cormorant Hat of my dear prince, alas!
So the great town of my dear prince was destroyed, alas!

Blinded by her tears and scarcely knowing where she went, Omen wandered away from the blackened, ash-shrouded ruins, singing her mourning song. Sometimes she saw a small white mouse; and when she did, she unthinkingly followed the little creature. For days and days and days she wandered, like someone in a dream.

When she came to a lake, she wandered on around it, still following the small white mouse. And when she came to a fire smouldering under the roots of a spruce tree, she sat down with her back to the fire, still singing her mourning song.

Now, AS IT HAPPENED, this fire was the funeral pyre of the only daughter of a chief and chieftainess from a coastal village down river from the lake. And the dead princess, too, had been of the Eagle Crest; she too had worn the great Eagle name of Omen.

As the live Omen was sitting there, singing her mourning song, a canoe from the village passed by. And seeing the girl sitting by the fire, the people in the canoe thought that *their* princess had come back to life. So they raced back to the village.

At once the chief and chieftainess came to the fire. When they saw the desolate princess, they too thought she was their daughter come back to life. Or perhaps they only chose to think so.

"My dear!" they murmured. "Are you indeed Omen?"

"I am Omen," the princess told them.

They took her back to their village, where they gave a feast and presented her to the people as their daughter brought back to life.

When Omen protested that she was not *that* princess, and when she did indeed seem ignorant of things *that* princess ought to have known, they said it was only because she had been for a time in the Land of Ghosts. Comforted by her presence, they chose not to believe her protests. When people wondered about the ash-smudged chief's fringed dancing blanket she wore, the chief and chieftainess said that, with one who had been in the spirit world, things could be beyond human explanation.

Caught in the web of false identity, Omen soon grew alert for a chance to escape; for she had an obligation to the Clan that had insured her survival. She had an obligation to the children who must one day wear their true names, and not the names of the dead princess's people. Names like Asdilda. Indeed, there *must* be another Asdilda, one who would wear a Cormorant Hat with proper respect and so bring back the favor of the spirit being it had honored.

One day, when the strawberries were ripe, Omen insisted on going with a group of young women who were to paddle to their favorite berry patch. Strangely, she also insisted on wearing her chief's fringed dancing blanket. Yet, when they arrived at the patch, she said she didn't wish to pick berries after all. She wished to stay on the beach. Alone!

The young women shrugged their shoulders at one another. They smiled indulgently at the confused girl who had returned from the Land of Ghosts. Then they left her on the beach. Alone.

As soon as they had disappeared along the trail to their berry patch, Omen quietly launched the canoe and paddled off toward an island. Her duty was to the royal bloodline she carried. She must find a place where she was accepted as herself. Her children must wear their true names and their true crests; they must sing their own songs and dance their own dances; they must fish and hunt in their own fishing stations, their own hunting grounds. They must claim the treasures that had been buried with her.

The wind was rising. But her obligation to the future of her own Eagle Clan made her dismiss her fears of a storm and paddle on. After all, she was Haida. She was one of the sea-roving lords of the coast. So she drove her canoe on, into the rising seas.

Suddenly, in the way of these northern waters, a storm struck. The wind whipped up into a fierce southwesterly gale. The princess was helpless as it blew her out into the open sea and swept her northeastward toward the mainland. As icy spray drenched her and terrifying waves threatened to engulf the canoe, she could only try to keep it heading into the seas. She could only go where the spirits sent her.

For a long, weary time, she went where the spirits sent her, always northeastward. She was close to the mainland before the gale blew itself out. So it was a young sea hunting chief of the mainland Tsimshians who finally saw her and came to her rescue. And when he had heard her story, he took her to his village and married her.

Since, by her noble bearing and costly ornaments, she was clearly the great Eagle princess she claimed to be, the people were happy about the marriage.

The young chief's two old wives were not. In the way of some of the Northern People, he had inherited his uncle's wives with his uncle's titles. And he had little love for either of them. When their sharp eyes saw that he had a great love for the beautiful young wife he had found for himself, they were consumed by jealousy. And they began to taunt Omen.

"You have no family!" they taunted her. "You have no honor and wealth to bring to the marriage." She was even a foreigner who could not speak their language properly. "Haida slave!" they taunted her.

Because she loved her husband, and because her duty was to have children who would wear the great names of her people, Omen endured their taunts in silence. But when her children began to grow up around her, she could not endure the taunts that had now turned in full fury against them.

"It is not to be borne!" she stormed at her husband. "My children must be treated with honor."

"Our children shall be treated with honor," he

promised. And he gave a great feast for the children. There, before the chiefs and people of many villages, they were ceremonially given the great Haida names they were entitled to wear, and the crests and songs and dances that went with the names. The eldest boy—Asdilda—was given a Cormorant Hat his father had had made for him, and a cane with a frog at the top and a frog at the bottom. The chief's fringed dancing blanket that his mother had taken from her ruined village was laid on his young shoulders.

Still there was no happy acceptance of their worth in their father's village. And there was no maternal uncle to take them away, as boys should be taken away, to their ancestral Haida village. Indeed there was no ancestral village, but only a desolation where the wind howled with the ghosts.

"Son of a Haida slave!" the jealous old wives continued to shriek at the new Asdilda whenever he chanced to go near them. And the tall youth narrowed his eyes in increasing fury.

"It is not to be borne!" Omen stormed again at her husband.

"It is not to be borne," he sadly agreed. And together they began to plan the return of the older children to their ancestral homeland across the sea, in the Haida islands. At the spring trading, they chose a magnificent Haida canoe decorated with the mighty Eagle. They secured costly garments for the young people and costly gifts for them to distribute when they had reached their ancestral homeland. They selected six stalwart slaves to man the canoe, and they provisioned it well for the journey.

Then, when the weather was right, they sent the four eldest children—three sons and a daughter—out across the sea where they had never been, southwestward to the Haida islands.

"Go and claim your birthright!" Omen said, embracing each of her departing children sadly. Who knew what would happen to them? Who knew when they would all meet again? "Your duty is toward the future, as mine is," she told them. "Go proudly, young Eagles!" For proper pride was a strength to young people. As false pride was a menace.

Almost blinded by her tears, Omen watched her children move out into the smooth, rolling swells of the mighty ocean. Remembering her own crossing of those perilous seas, she scanned the sky with anxious eyes; she scattered eagle down—the symbol of peace and friendship—on the often stormy waters.

"Go proudly, young Eagles!" she murmured into the wind.

As THEIR MAGNIFICENT CANOE neared the village where Omen had once been held by the chief and chieftainess who had lost their own daughter, the young people waved cedar boughs and scattered eagle down to show they came in peace.

Wearing the old chief's fringed dancing blanket and the new Cormorant Hat, Asdilda stood high on a plank that had been laid across the canoe. And when the people of the village had gathered warily on the beach, he called out, "Was a princess lost from this village, many years ago, when the young women went to pick strawberries?"

Warriors stood, alert and watching, while the people answered, "Yes!"

"We are Omen's children!" Asdilda called out. "Returned to find our own ancestral village that was burned by the fury of Volcano Woman."

The people knew of the village that had been burned by the fury of Volcano Woman. They had heard of the things the vanished princess had claimed. So they welcomed her children with a great feast. And Asdilda presented costly gifts his parents had sent with him.

Then the marveling people went with Omen's children to guide them to the burned-out village. And when the canoes had reached it, the people watched while Asdilda and his brothers and his slaves uncovered the secret chamber in the blackened ruins of the biggest house. They cheered as the great coppers were lifted out, and the great wealth chests full of costly garments.

Indeed it was true—what the confused girl had once said and what her son had repeated. Truly these were royal Haida Eagles returned to claim their birthright. Eagles from many villages would help them rebuild the village. And marriages would be arranged. For a people's duty was always to the future.

THERE WAS HAPPINESS in the big, busy mouse eyes that watched as the new Asdilda claimed his ancestral rights. Clearly *he* would be worthy of the great hat he wore.

Still, Mouse Woman decided, she would keep an eye on him and on his brothers and his sister. For *any* young person could encounter a trickster narnauk and need help to keep everything equal.

There might yet be wool in it for her ravelly little fingers.

The Princess Who Rejected Her Cousin

Nothing caused more muddleheadedness than love and marriage, Mouse Woman decided one day as she watched the world with her big, busy mouse eyes.

"Young people ought to do the proper thing," she squeaked indignantly to herself. The proper thing, of course, was to let their relatives make all the decisions about anything as important as marriage.

"No good ever comes of interfering with the proper way," she told herself. And her nose twitched as she thought of how a certain princess was interfering with the marriage arrangements her relatives were making for her.

"No good will come of this interfering," Mouse Woman squeaked. And being the busiest little busybody in the Place of Supernatural Beings, she intended to do a little interfering herself. Just to keep everything equal, of course.

IT WAS ALL HAPPENING in a certain village where there were only two chiefs: a man and his sister, both of the Eagle Crest.

The man was married to a great lady of the Wolf Crest. So, in the way of this matrilineal society, his son was Wolf Crest, like the mother; while his sister's daughter was Eagle Crest, like *her* mother. And this was all very convenient for the relatives on both sides. The two young people were of suitably similar high rank, and of suitably different crests. Clearly, the proper thing was for the cousins to marry one another.

The Wolf Prince was delighted with the arrangement, for he loved his beautiful cousin.

It was the Eagle Princess who was causing all the trouble. She did not want to marry her cousin, however high-ranking and worthy he might be. There were handsomer princes in other villages, she knew; and any of them would want to marry a princess as beautiful as herself. "So why should I marry him?" she asked the girls who were her friends-and-attendants.

"You will marry the Wolf Prince!" her relatives told her.

"I won't!" she told them. She flatly rejected her cousin. But she did not tell him that. Instead, she decided to make a fool of him.

One evening, after he had arrived from the village where he now lived with his uncle, a great Wolf chief, she dressed herself in her finest woolen robes and ear ornaments. She strolled through the village where the lovesick youth was sure to see her. Then, strolling on to a certain tree beyond the village, she sent her girls back to invite him to come to her. And when he had come, she held out her arms and embraced him.

Since it was the first time she had ever embraced him, the lovesick youth was wildly happy. "Marry me soon!" he urged her.

"As soon as I'm sure you really love me," she answered, smiling wistfully at him. "But how can I be sure you're not marrying me just because it's been arranged by your relatives?"

"You can be sure," he told her. "And if you can't be sure, let me prove my love! I would do anything for you."

"Anything?" she challenged him, running her fingers over his right cheek as if she loved him dearly. "Would you slash this cheek for me?"

"Slash my cheek!" he protested, aghast at such a suggestion. But by the time she had run her fingers several more times over his cheek, the lovesick youth said, "I'll slash my cheek if that's the only way I can prove my love." And that very night he slashed his right cheek.

"Now do you believe I love you?" he asked her the next evening, when he met her once more by the tree.

"More than I did before," she admitted. She

embraced him as though *she* loved *him* dearly. Yet there was still doubt in her eyes as she ran her fingers over his left cheek.

"What more can I do to prove my love?" he demanded.

"Well . . ." she said, still running her fingers over his left cheek as though *she* loved *him* dearly. "You could slash this cheek too."

"But why?" he protested.

"Just to prove that you love me," she told him. And so wistful did she seem, and so fond of him, that the lovesick youth was ready to do *anything* to prove his love and hasten the marriage. That very night he slashed his left cheek.

"Now do you believe I love you?" he asked her the next evening, when he met her once more by the tree.

"More than I did before," she admitted. She embraced him as though *she* loved *him* dearly. Yet there was still doubt in her eyes as she ran her fingers through his long glossy black hair.

"What more can I do to prove my love?" he demanded.

"Well . . ." she said, still running her fingers through his long glossy black hair, "You could cut off your hair."

"My hair!" he protested. For only slaves had their heads shorn. "Why should I cut off my hair?"

"Just to prove that you love me," she told him. And so wistful did she seem, and so fond of him, that the lovesick youth was ready to do *anything* to prove his love and hasten the marriage. That very night he cut off his long glossy black hair.

"Now do you believe I love you?" he asked her the next evening, when he met her once more by the tree. "Haven't I proved that I love you?"

"You have proved that you are a fool!" she told him with flashing eyes. "And I can't make myself ridiculous by marrying a fool—a fool with two slashed cheeks and hair cut off like a slave's hair!" She turned indignantly from him and made her way to the village.

The Wolf Prince was desolated. He had indeed proved that he was a fool. And there would be nothing now for him in the village except ridicule. His cousin had never intended to marry him. She had only wanted to make a fool of him.

Shrinking with shame, the once proud prince raced off along the trail to the north, not knowing or caring where he went. All he wanted was to get away from the girl who had made him ridiculous.

For three days he went on, not knowing or caring where he went. On the fourth day, he came upon a little lame mouse trying to climb over a log.

"Poor little mouse!" he said; for he could never be so lost in his own troubles that he couldn't see the troubles of others. He lifted it gently over the log and watched it with compassionate eyes as it disappeared into a thicket of tall ferns.

Then he heard a voice call out from behind the ferns. "Come in, dear Prince!" the voice invited, in small but imperious squeaks.

Surprised by the command, the Wolf Prince parted the ferns. And there, to his amazement, was a house decorated with Mouse totems.

"Come in, dear Prince!" the imperious little voice repeated.

He went in. And there was the tiniest grandmother he had ever seen. She had a field mouse robe on her little shoulders.

"Mouse Woman!" he cried out. And now his eyes shone. For it was well known that Mouse Woman was a friend to young people who'd been tricked into trouble.

"Sit down, dear Prince!" she invited. "You have been kind to me, so I shall repay your kindness." She was watching the swing of his sea shell ear ornaments, for it was wool that swung the sea shells.

The Wolf Prince sat down on a mat by the fire. And he gratefully took the roasted salmon the tiny narnauk gave him. "I have proved myself a fool," he said, unhappily.

"Not so great a fool as the young woman who wanted to prove you one," Mouse Woman told him. And her nose twitched. "You will prove *that* when you go back to her village."

He shrank back at the very thought of a return

to that village. "I can't go back looking like a fool and a slave," he protested.

"No need, if you take my advice," Mouse Woman assured him.

He pulled a woolen fringe from his belt and gave it to the tiny narnauk. For it was well known that, with Mouse Woman, if advice were to be given, something must be given in return.

While her ravelly little fingers were tearing at the wool, Mouse Woman gave him the advice he needed. "Stay on the trail until you come to a brook," she told him. "Once across the brook, you will see the large house of Chief Pestilence."

"Chief Pestilence?" he said, trying not to shrink back from the very name.

"When you near the house, call out in a loud voice, "I come to be made beautiful in the house of Pestilence!"

Hiding his horror, the Wolf Prince repeated the words, "I come to be made beautiful in the house of Pestilence!"

"But beware!" Mouse Woman warned, holding up a finger. "There will be many there who will entice you to go with them. But do not listen to them! For they would make you what they are—maimed. Listen to no one but Chief Pestilence!"

"I will listen to no one but Chief Pestilence," he promised. He had had enough of people enticing him only to do him injury.

After he had slept and eaten again, the Wolf

Prince went on his way. He had not gone far before he came to a brook. And after he had crossed it, he saw a large house, as Mouse Woman had said he would. So he walked toward it, calling out in a loud voice, "I come to be made beautiful in the house of Pestilence!" When he reached the door, he went in.

At once, from all sides, people beckoned to him and called out, "Come this way! Come this way!" Many of them were beautiful women, enticing him, "Come this way! Come this way!" But as he stayed by the door, watching them, he saw that—as Mouse Woman had warned!—many of them were maimed.

At last Chief Pestilence and his beautiful daughter came from a room at the rear of the house.

"Come this way, dear Prince!" the Chief invited.

Moving through the now silent people, the Wolf Prince went to the rear of the house and sat down on the mat indicated.

"Fetch the water!" the Chief ordered his attendants.

Soon an enormous wooden tub was filled with water that started to heat of itself. Steam began rising from it.

"Put the prince into the water!" the Chief ordered.

The Wolf Prince gasped. For the water had begun to boil. Yet he made no protest as he was put into it. Then he lay as though dead.

When the water had stopped boiling and the dross had been strained off, the prince was lifted out and laid on a plank. Then, chanting and shaking his carved rattle, Chief Pestilence jumped over the body. His daughter, too, jumped over it.

The Wolf Prince stirred. He opened his eyes and sat up. In wonderment! For his scars were healed. His skin shone like the skin of a Supernatural Being. But his head was still shorn, like a slave's head.

"Fetch my comb!" Chief Pestilence ordered. And when he began to comb the stubble of hair, the hair grew until it was a long glossy black mane hanging down to the youth's hips.

"Now be on your way!" said Chief Pestilence.

Beautiful and shining as a supernatural being, the Wolf Prince almost raced back to the village where he had proved himself a fool. And there the people who had given him up for lost were themselves lost, in wonderment. "What happened to you?" they asked him.

"I was made beautiful in the house of Pestilence," he told them. And he told them little more of what had happened to him. Only that after four days of travel on the northern trail, Mouse Woman had directed him to a large house across a brook. "I went into the house crying out in a loud voice, 'I come to be made beautiful in the house of Pestilence!' I was put into a tub of hot water. And I came out healed and shining." Since the whole subject was painful to him, that is all he told them.

For days the villagers marvelled over what had happened to him, while the Eagle Princess waited for him to come to her. Now that he was the handsomest of all the princes in all the villages, she wanted to marry him. "Now that he has returned," she told her relatives, "we must get on with the marriage you arranged for us."

But the once lovesick youth said nothing about the marriage. He made no move to see the Eagle Princess.

At last, in despair, she sent her maid to him.

"My mistress wishes you to come to her," the maid said. "For she loves you dearly."

"Oh, I don't think she loves me dearly," the prince answered.

"Truly she does!" the maid exclaimed, as she had been instructed to exclaim. "She would do anything to prove her love for you!"

"Indeed?" he said. "Would she slash her beautiful right cheek to prove her love?"

"I . . . will . . . ask her," the maid said, thinking of what would happen *when* she asked her.

"Slash my cheek?" the Eagle Princess screamed, striking the poor maid with battering blows. But when she had calmed down, she remembered that the Wolf Prince was handsomer after his mutilations than he had been before them. "Well . . . if that is the only way I can prove my love . . ."

she said. And that very night she slashed her right cheek.

"Now will you come to my mistress?" the maid begged the Wolf Prince the next day. "For she loves you dearly. She has slashed her right cheek to prove her love."

"But does she love me enough to slash her other cheek?" the once lovesick youth asked.

"I . . . will . . . ask her," the maid said, thinking of what would happen *when* she asked her.

"Slash my other cheek?" the Eagle Princess screamed, striking the poor maid with battering blows. But when she had calmed down and thought about it, she slashed her other cheek.

"Now will you come to my mistress?" the maid begged the Wolf Prince the next day. "For she loves you dearly. She has slashed her other cheek to prove her love."

"But would she cut off her hair for me, as I cut off mine to prove that *I* loved *her?"* he asked.

"I . . . will . . . ask her," the maid said, again thinking of what would happen *when* she asked her.

"Cut off my hair?" the Eagle Princess screamed, striking the poor maid with many battering blows. "My beautiful long glossy black hair!" But when she had calmed down and thought about it, she cut off her long glossy black hair.

"*Now* will you come to my mistress?" the poor maid begged. And truly she wished he would come before she herself had been battered to bits. "She has done everything you asked, to prove how dearly she loves you. She wants you to marry her."

"Marry a lady with slashed cheeks?" the Wolf prince said, aghast at such a suggestion. "With hair cut off like a slave's hair! How could she think I would make myself ridiculous by marrying such a lady?"

This time the poor maid scarcely dared to go back and face the anger of the rejected princess. "He says . . . he will not . . . marry a lady with slashed cheeks," she whimpered as she tried to dodge the angriest of the blows, "and hair . . . cut off like a slave's hair." She fled from the house before she could be battered to bits.

The Eagle Princess was furious. And now she was ashamed to venture out into the village. For she had made herself ridiculous. But she would soon regain her beauty, she thought. Indeed she would increase her beauty as the Wolf Prince had increased his.

"Tonight, when it is dark," she told her maid, "we shall follow the trail to the north until we come to the house of Pestilence." She knew it was a large house across a brook, a house they would reach after four days of travel.

That night, when it was dark, the two of them slipped silently out of the house and made their way along the trail to the north. For three days they travelled. And on the fourth day, they came upon a little lame mouse trying to climb over a log.

"Stupid thing!" the princess said, kicking it from the side of the trail. Then she went on her way, watching for the brook they must cross.

By evening they came to the brook. And after they had crossed it, they saw the large house they were looking for. As they walked toward it, the Eagle Princess called out in a loud voice, "I come to be made beautiful in the house of Pestilence!" When she reached the house, she went in.

At once, from all sides, people beckoned to her and called out, "Come this way! Come this way!" Many of them were handsome men, enticing her, "Come this way! Come this way!"

And now, unwarned of any danger, the princess went one way while her maid went another. The maimed people fell on both of them. Several slashed at the princess and broke one of her bones, while others battered the poor maid.

Somehow, the two managed to escape. And with the maid almost carrying the princess, they hobbled back along the trail. But now it was a long, long, weary, painful way. Day after day after day after day they hobbled along. When they neared the village, the princess began to shrink back at the thought of returning there ugly and ragged and crippled. Before they reached it, she died of shame, right there on the trail.

The poor maid—dismayed by everything that had happened, and almost battered to bits even on the way home—hobbled on to the village to tell her mistress's family

"THIS IS WHAT COMES of allowing young people to interfere with marriage arrangements," people told one another when the wailing for the princess was over.

So they made a strict rule.

"In future, when all the relatives have agreed on a certain marriage, THE YOUNG PEOPLE WILL MARRY THE ONES CHOSEN FOR THEM!"

"NOW THERE WILL BE no more muddleheadedness about love and marriage," Mouse Woman squeaked to herself. And with much pleasure she watched relatives make arrangements for the marriage of the Wolf Prince to a beautiful Bear Princess from another village.

The invisible little narnauk watched as the princess was brought to the prince's village seated on a ceremonial plank that had been laid across two magnificent canoes filled with costly gifts and with joyously chanting relatives.

Then for three days she watched as the prince and the princess sat by the fire trying to *keep* their dignity while the rest of the young people laughed and joked and played pranks trying to make them *lose* their dignity. For it was all part of the proper way to conduct a marriage.

Indeed, there was no way like the *proper way* of doing things, Mouse Woman thought as she scurried home from the wedding.

"Now there will be no more muddleheadedness about love and marriage," she told herself again, in small but imperious squeaks.

Still, she would keep on watching the world with her big, busy mouse eyes. For, however properly things were arranged for them, young people would sometimes be muddleheads. Somehow, sooner or later, they would get themselves into trouble. And then they would need a friend's help to keep everything equal in the world of human beings and narnauks.

Story Sources

DURING THE PAST two centuries, the rich native cultures of our Northwest Coast have almost vanished into the more dominant immigrant cultures. Fortunately for us, there have always been people concerned to record the stories before they were forgotten.

Mouse Woman has been waiting for us to find her in the following collections.

1899. *Tales from the Totems of the Hidery,* collected by James Deans for the Archives of the International Folk-lore Association.

1905. *Haida Texts,* collected by John Reed Swanton for the Jessup North Pacific Expedition publications, Memoirs of the American Museum of Natural History.

1908. *The Koryak,* collected by Waldemar Jochelson for The Jessup North Pacific Expedition publications, Memoirs of the American Museum of Natural History.

1909–1910. *Tsimshian Myths,* collected by Franz Boas for the Thirty-First Annual Report of the Bureau of American Ethnology to the Secretary of the Smithsonian Institution.

1953. *Haida Myths Illustrated in Argillite Carvings,* by Marius Barbeau, Bulletin No. 127, Anthropological Series No. 32, National Museum of Canada.